High Five

a Montbretia Armstrong novella

Simon Cann

Coombe
Hill
Publishing

Published by Coombe Hill Publishing
33 Melrose Gardens
New Malden
Surrey KT3 3HQ
United Kingdom
coombehillpublishing.com

ISBN: 978-1-910398-08-1 (paperback)
ISBN: 978-1-910398-09-8 (ePub)

A big thank you to:

- Cathleen Small for her editorial input.

- Sarah Kruger (sarahkrugerdesigns.com) for the cover art.

one

Somewhere behind the noise of the city there was a beat.

Somewhere there was a beat floating through the hum of the warm spring evening: the traffic, the bars with their music blaring, the people on the street shouting, laughing. Visitors from out of town—not tourists as such, but visitors from the convention centers, kicking loose on the limit of their expenses after a day spent at conferences with titles like Global Strategic Sourcing and Procurement Summit, or WiFi and Small Cells World Summit, or my favorite, Light-Sheet Fluorescence Microscopy International Conference, whatever that meant. Somewhere beyond that noise of the city, there was the rhythm of a drummer.

No. Not *a* drummer: two drummers.

Two drummers, outside.

"So now you're saying I should behave like a tourist?" I asked.

It wasn't so much a question as an attempt to take an innocent comment Curtis had made and provoke.

He turned to face me. His head did that strange rocking thing it did when he tried to keep walking straight. When most people turn to face you and keep walking, their head moves at a consistent speed. Not so with Curtis—with his limp, his head would move quickly when he took a step with his good leg, but slower as he limped with his other leg.

Against his dark skin the two white orbs, each with a black iris making contact, suggested he was acknowledging me.

"I'm not a tourist, but you take me to one of the main tourist traps in Barcelona."

Without saying anything, he turned back to face the direction we were walking. Not that my question required a response—he knew I was trying to needle him, but he also knew that he had won: I was here, and the Sagrada Família was within a few minutes. I was fully committed to the mission or whatever it was Curtis liked to say when he did his soldier-boy-speak.

And now that I had the time to think about it, I actually quite liked the idea of a evening visit to the Sagrada Família—the cathedral designed by Antoni Gaudí, where construction began in 1882 but has still not been completed today, some 130 years later. But I wasn't going to tell Curtis that, since I was still committed to my mission of trying to get a rise out of him.

After all, this was meant to be my night off. My first night in nearly two weeks that I wasn't working at the bar.

I was going to do some washing—maybe I could get two loads done—and perhaps watch a movie. Someone had piggybacked a cable onto the satellite from the apartment on the top floor, and sometimes there were decent movies in English. And sometimes the signal just got scrambled.

"You do know I've been here before, Curtis," I said, exaggerating the "urrrrrrr" in Curtis because I knew that bugged him. "Several times." Still no response. "When I go and see my sister in London I don't go to Buckingham Palace, the Tower of London, the Houses of Parliament, and Westminster Abbey *every* time."

His face softened. When he talked, his voice was calm, conciliatory, with a slight hint of wonder. "But when did you last come here at night...after dark...just to sit and watch?" He carried on before I could reply. "It's different at night. Better. You haven't got the blazing sky to blind you. You can look up at the towers and see the detail. It really looks like it's melting. Take some photos—it's something to write about on your blog."

He was trying to appeal to my emotional side, but all he had done was give me ammunition. "You say take photos? Now? Now, after I've left my camera in the apartment?" He didn't react. "You didn't think to mention that before we left?"

There was a tightening in his jaw. I took that as regret. Even if it wasn't, I was happy to give him the benefit of my doubt.

Like me, he probably didn't think about it because we had left the apartment quickly. Curtis got a call. He didn't say who had called, but he was suddenly really keen for me to join him. And as soon as I gave way and agreed to come, we left. No pause. No hesitation. We were heading for the door.

Well, there was a pause. "Put your...you know...zip purse thing under your blouse." That delayed us by thirty seconds at most as I stepped into my room, unbuttoned my blouse, got one arm out of the sleeve to get the purse strapped across my chest, and started to re-button. As we left the apartment—before I had fastened all the buttons and as I tried to untangle the lanyard around my neck holding my phone, which was caught in the buttons—he said, "Slip that in the purse," and passed me a small envelope, little bigger than a credit card and feeling as if it contained a credit card.

Curtis made no attempt at explanation.

As we left the apartment, Curtis picked up my jacket. We got to the street and started to walk through the residential backstreets, the apartment blocks looming over both sides. It was warm enough that I didn't need my jacket at that moment. However, I did want it with me for when the temperature fell, so I was happy for Curtis to carry it.

After a few minutes, Curtis flipped my jacket over his shoulder. "I'm Montbretia," he said, his voice high and squeaky, "but you can call me Monty. Look at my hair, it's so shiny."

I didn't react, but I did remember. And as the sound of drumming got louder I thought about payback.

This kind of rhythm wasn't indigenous to Barcelona. Or Europe. This wasn't the rhythm of snare drums played by soldiers—this wasn't any kind of drum played with sticks. It wasn't the kind of drums I had heard in the South American carnivals. This was the sound of Africa. But in Barcelona, on a spring evening.

This beat was two people who since birth had known rhythm as a part of their culture. Two who knew the joy of rhythm and could communicate through beats. This was rhythm being played with hands—palms, fingers, knuckles making contact with animal skins drawn tight over a hollow tube.

This wasn't the four-on-the-floor that you heard in the bars and clubs around Barcelona, especially down by the docks—the kind of electronic dance music that numbs you into hypnosis through its repetition. This was something with a life of its own. It breathed, in and out. One part subtly faster while the counter-rhythm slowed. Each delicate change shifting the beat, and yet making it impossible not to move your body to the rhythm.

As we walked, I became aware of people being affected by the rhythm. Some walked to the beat. Others swayed or half-danced. I could feel my ass as if it had a life of its own, submitting to the involuntary instruction to sway as my feet matched their pace to follow the pulse.

And there was singing—or more accurately, chanting. A male voice leading, with others following like a rhythmic echo: a choir and drums.

But one person didn't seem to be affected by the rhythm. One person seemed to be oblivious to even the presence of drummers. One person: Curtis.

Currrrrtis.

I started to plot how I could bug him next. He deserved it: He had ruined my evening of doing nothing apart from my laundry and chilling in front of the TV, and he had asked me to carry an envelope.

Asked me to carry an envelope...and yet, he was happy to carry my jacket, his own wallet, which I presumed had far more valuable contents, and also his door key. Now sure, he could've asked me to put his wallet in my purse, but the bulge would have given me a third boob.

Third boob or not, it would have been petty of me not to carry the envelope. As someone who had taken action to mitigate the effect of crime. After all, I was the girl without a smartphone. I was the girl who made her sister buy a smartphone, but for myself, I had a plain old candy-bar phone that wouldn't have looked out of place twenty years ago. It was great for making calls and a bit of a fiddle for sending texts, but it worked, and it would happily hang from a lanyard around my neck.

If the phone got stolen—not that anyone would steal one of these old phones—then I didn't care. I still had a stack of them that I had collected from friends when they got smartphones. In the last two years, I've gone through about three phones, and none of them has cost me anything.

The drums were getting closer—two drums from two players. There were different—but interlocking—rhythms. The deeper-pitched drum was playing more of a rhythmic beat. The higher-pitched drum was playing the fills. Between the two a call and response mirrored by the chanting: one man calling, the group responding.

As we took the corner, near the five-way junction with a café on the apex, the musicians came into view. Two men with drums, three maybe four dancing and chanting. I say dancing, but it was more of a shuffle with movement from the torso and upward.

"Fucking beggars," spat Curtis under his breath as he looked up to see the group of musicians. "They're just fucking beggars. Come on, this way." He pointed his head across the street away from the noisy group.

"Oh no," I said, trying to keep the grin off my face. "No, no, no. No, you don't get to make that choice. You take me out for a bit of sightseeing—you're not going to stop me from behaving like a tourist."

"Monty, no. They're criminals who just happen to have some musical talent." His voice started as a command, but there was a mixture of annoyance and frustration in his tone as he continued. I wasn't sure whether that was because of his distaste for the musical street-hustlers or because he knew I was yanking his chain, and from the way the rhythm was moving my ass, he knew I was about to yank his chain harder.

He was right: These probably were criminal beggars masquerading as street entertainers. Instinctively, I put my hand to my chest to check the lanyard holding my phone and the purse under my blouse.

But I probably didn't need to worry—for these so-called street entertainers, I guessed their main objective was the business crowd, and there's always a conference in Barcelona. When you're done with your day talking about white goods and accessories for a kitchen that have no real-world use or the latest electronic gizmos, what do you do in Barcelona? You go for tapas, then hit the bars and clubs, and find a whore near the docks. As long as you're back at your conference by the time the boss speaks, no one really cares what you do on your own time.

The drummers seemed to be heading toward the docks to find the drunk businessmen and -women. The visitors were sure to be taken in by the apparent culture while their guard was dulled by alcohol and the need to make sure everyone with them knew that they were kicking loose and having a *great* time.

As we moved closer—the drums loud enough that all I could hear were the drums and the chanting...no sounds of the passing cars—my hand involuntarily went to again check my phone's lanyard and the purse under my blouse, but this time I started to feel self-conscious. Was I just drawing attention to what I thought had value?

Curtis caught my eye. The annoyance and the disapproval were clear. I had hit my target. He took me sightseeing, and now I was going to behave like a tourist and allow myself to be subsumed into the world of African street entertainers.

The leader was standing Christ-like, arms outstretched, head back, chanting to the night sky. His only movement— apart from his lower jaw—was his shoulders lifting, then dropping as if expelling extra air to add emphasis to the beats. Under the streetlight, his white robe glistened. This was more than plain cotton, although the design of the garment, along with the simple hat perched on his head and the sandals on his feet, implied a humility that didn't accord with his performance.

As the Christ-like leader chanted to the heavens, his acolytes followed. One with a poorly fitting green-and-orange-checkered robe that was too short and showed his jeans and sneakers, echoed the leader—his chants harmonizing. A third man in a flowing red robe, with a plunging V-shaped ornate green collar with gold stitching, made a series of rhythmic grunts, a rainbow of nuanced sounds, each with its own rhythm and forming part of the orchestration.

A fourth man in a royal-blue jacket and pants combination started to circle the group as it subsumed me and Curtis in the middle. While we became the center of their focus, the man in blue continued with a range of animal-like screeches and howls, all perfectly in time and rhythm with the drums.

By now my ass was moving like it had a mind of its own. The drummers pounded out the rhythm, my ass moved, and my head and shoulders bobbed—within the circle the evening had become ten degrees warmer, and any notion of a slight chill from the early spring breeze coming off the Mediterranean was gone.

The guy in the red robe moved closer—of the four without drums, he was the one closest to dancing, although his movements seemed more intended to mirror mine. He smiled broadly, a row of ivory across his near-black skin. As he moved closer, he exaggerated the sway of his hips, pushing his ass farther toward me with each beat as he turned his body to stand by my side, seemingly cautious not to invade my personal space.

The drummers were playing louder, faster. Everywhere I looked I was seeing colors and textures I had never seen before as I swirled into this new world. There was a bump against my ass. I turned, slightly surprised. The ivory grin told me it was intended, and our eyes met momentarily. I bumped back and looked to Curtis.

With his injured leg that led to his limp, his movement was restricted. This didn't worry me—it wasn't as if I ever wanted to go out clubbing—but it did limit how well he could pretend that he wasn't fussed by the attention we were getting. If you can jig in some sort of fashion, it's far less noticeable than if you just stand still and scowl, which was what Curtis was doing. He could get away without nimble footwork, but he wasn't even moving his shoulders.

My ass was bumped again, gently. And again—this time, the contact lingered. I turned to the man in the red robe and saw the ivory smile from the polished ebony face. I looked down to his shoulder, which was rolling forward. When he saw he had my attention, he rolled his left shoulder forward once, then his right, and back to his left, continuing with an almost hypnotic regularity that synchronized with the beat of the drums.

Seeing my attention was focused, he held his hands in front of him, rolling them forward and shrugging his nearest shoulder to encourage me to follow. As I hesitatingly shadowed, he slowed to mirror my rhythm, pushing me gradually to pick up the pace—his smiling mouth hanging open as he added to the chorus of chants.

Slowly he started to lift his rolling hands. I matched. As my hands got higher, they separated until I had one hand rolling forward in front of each shoulder. A huge grin spread across his face, and he bumped my ass again.

Sheepishly, I looked away to see Curtis remaining angry and motionless. The guy in the green-and-orange-checkered robe had placed himself between us, standing to my side but directly behind Curtis, gently nudging him as if encouraging him to join in. Up close he was shorter, with dull charcoal skin that seemed to have aged. He nudged Curtis, then turned and smiled at me, revealing yellowed teeth with gaps.

The encouragement had no effect on Curtis, who was

slowly radiating anger. That ire was likely to combust if the Christ-like guy in white, who was moving toward him, took him in hand to try to force him to dance.

There was damp perspiration on my brow as my hands continued to roll forward at my shoulders. I wasn't sure whether this was physical exertion or nervous energy, but in either case, my newfound attendants seemed ready to deal with my every dance-related need.

I looked back to Curtis. The white robe was in front of him. He looked to Curtis, to me, then back to Curtis, "She is beautiful. High five!" He held up his hand to high five Curtis. Curtis left him hanging.

It felt like a hand touching my ass.

My head shot to the right. The guy in red had his hands in front of him. To the right—the guy in green and orange was jostling up behind Curtis.

"She is the most beautiful woman I have ever seen. High five!" The black Christ-like figure in white spoke with the accent of someone brought up in a former British colonial country. Proper English, but somehow a learned precision against a heavy accent—there was nothing natural, nothing suggesting this was how he spoke. And this was nothing like the stick-up-the-ass of the English Received Pronunciation.

"High five, my friend, high five," said the man in white in his obsequious English-miming accent, holding his hand up to take Curtis's high five.

Both of Curtis's arms remained resolutely by his side. The guy in the green and orange robe leaned over Curtis, jostling him forward, before he took the high five and then pulled at Curtis's arm, trying to get him to join in.

My ass was bumped again. I went to smile at the guy in red, but he seemed to be paying attention to whatever was going on with Curtis. My head continued to turn until I noticed the drummer who was playing the smaller drum. He had moved up close behind me and was hunched over his drum, jigging on the spot: two steps left, two steps right, right-knee lifted as he ducked his head, two steps back, seemingly lost in his own world and clearly unaware that he had bumped me.

Back toward Curtis; his eyes were flashing, trying to take in the situation as he was being crowded from his last free side by the other drummer—this one playing the large drum—his face humorless.

There was a hand on my ass again. As I turned, I saw the guy in the blue suit continuing his path around our gathering, clucking and barking as he went.

There was a tapping on my shoulder: The drummer behind me was playing one rhythm on his drum and another on my back. It was a gentle beat, soft, the lightest of tapping on my back. Each new tap in a different position, as if intended to ensure no pain.

And on my shoulder, another beat began. The guy in the red robe smiled and looked me straight in the eye, his head cocked slightly, questioning...asking permission. My laugh was all he needed.

I could feel a hand sliding around my waist from the other side. I tried to wiggle it away—I don't know why, but I felt less comfortable about being touched, and touched in that way, by the guy in the green-and-orange-checkered robe. There was something about the decaying teeth that turned me off.

The hand was withdrawn, but the beats on my back continued and spread. The drummer was now using both hands, gently beating on my back, my shoulders, and occasionally bending over to beat on my thighs before righting himself.

The hand was back. It was around my waist with the attached hand holding me around the side. Not tightly—but the hand was there. Not on my hip, but more around my waist. I knew what would happen: If I pulled away, the hand would slip and slip upward. My right boob would get groped, and he would say it was my fault.

And unfortunately, basic mechanics would support his contention even if the law wouldn't. With an arm fixed at the shoulder and being a finite length, if I moved away, the arm would get pulled tighter, and his reaction would be to grip tighter. The arm would then slide up. Couple an arm moving up with a tighter grip, and there would be a lingering few seconds when he'd get a handful. Clearly this guy was a breast man, not a bum man or a leg man.

I reached, sliding my thumb down my chest, and unpeeled his fingers one by one, letting the hand drop to then brush past my ass.

But now the drummer was getting frisky—the rhythm included the occasional beat on my ass, and Mister Green and Orange was joining in with the drumming too...but only with one hand as his other slipped around my waist at the front.

"Hey!" I said. "Careful."

Curtis looked across. I knew that look—it wasn't anger anymore, it was concern.

The drummer had a new pattern; he seemed to be drumming a pattern that followed my bra. I hoped he wasn't one of those guys who thought it was funny to unhook bras. And the hand had returned, this time over my stomach, snagging my blouse where the purse lay under the cloth. Between them they could see what I was wearing and they had felt what I was wearing underneath, and there was a hand on my ass again. Not playing a rhythm—this was resting. Feeling. Evaluating. Enjoying.

I wasn't sure who I was talking to, but my voice had an ugly tone: "I'm going to make this very clear. Get your hands off my ass or I'm gonna break your fingers. One by one."

The man in white threw back his head, laughing—his yellowing teeth gleaming against his black skin—as he faced Curtis. "She is a spirited girl you have there, sir. High five!" He confidently thrust his hand forward. Curtis again refused, a look of deepening concern having taken up residence on his face.

A hand landed on my ass again—a low-pitched slap. I let out a yelp as I became aware that an arm had snaked around my waist again. I grabbed a finger and pulled it back.

Although that hand was moving, it felt like there were other hands over my body—on my ass, on my breasts, slipping into my pockets, slipping between the buttons on my blouse. I twisted the finger and felt the hand leave my waist.

"She is a fighter, sir. High five!" Curtis ignored the man—his gaze was fixed on me.

There was a hand in the front pocket of my jeans. "Hey!"

Curtis heard the tension in my voice. Tension, or was it panic?

For the first time since we had been subsumed within the group, Curtis lifted his arms and pushed the man in the green-and-orange-checked robe out of the way and threw his arms around me. He was jostled from behind...and then there were these kids.

There were probably only four or five kids—all short, no more than eight or ten years old, and all with dark skins like the musicians—but all moving quickly, making it impossible to count their numbers as they weaved. One went in and out, one up and down, and a third circled us before trying to push between Curtis and me.

"Are you okay?" asked Curtis, pulling me tighter.

I didn't know what the answer was. All I knew was that I had started to cry. Curtis lowered his embrace and bear-hugged me, lifting me and using me as a battering ram to push outside of the circle. There were hands over me, and we were jostled. It felt like we were moving through a crowd of hundreds, not a group of seven adults and five kids.

There was a chill, and I could hear the musicians' noise becoming softer as Curtis lowered me, quietly whispering: "It's okay, you're safe now. It's alright, they're gone, and you're safe."

two

At a guess, we'd been there for fifteen minutes, and Curtis hadn't let go of me. He hadn't let go of me from the moment he carried me out of the circle of drummers where I'd been groped and pawed at by what felt like half of the street musician population of Barcelona.

Now, as I sat still, the spring night was chilly. I thought I was shivering. I wasn't; I was trembling, and even though I knew I was trembling, I wasn't quite sure how I felt.

It should be obvious—you get groped by a bunch of strangers in the street...that's a bad thing, right? And it was. But it hadn't started off that way—it had been just a bit of fun and an attempt to annoy Curtis—and I had been a willing participant. I was the one who dragged Curtis into the center as the drummers beat out a rhythm around us and the other guys chanted. And I'd given my agreement—tacit agreement—to the guy in the red robe.

And I had been enjoying myself. But then they went too far.

"Are you sure you're okay?" asked Curtis again. He held my right hand between both of his.

I nodded and tried to smile.

We sat on a bench in a park opposite the Sagrada Família. Where the church stood on its own—the views of it seemingly having been cleared from all sides—the park was surrounded by a mishmash of apartment blocks with stores and eateries at ground level.

Apart from us, the other occupants of the park seemed to be early season tourists all remaining on the designated path—no one had jumped the fences to the grass areas. There were couples where the men—always the men—brandished big cameras that they thought said, "I think I'm serious about photography; you should respect me as an artist." In truth, all they said was, "I'm a bit of a dick with more money than sense, and I've found an excuse to buy yet more gadgets that I don't need." For most of the other tourists, a cell phone was a satisfactory camera, especially for selfies that everyone without a big camera seemed to be taking.

It used to be that a ring on a finger would identify couples. Now, the way to identify couples was by looking at who was in the selfie. People who took selfies of, literally, themselves were on their own, even if they were with a group of friends—where the group selfies came later. The couples, however, were intent on taking selfies of themselves standing in front of the Sagrada Família in order to prove to their Facebook friends and their former partners stalking them on Facebook that they were a happy couple enjoying themselves and doing cool things. After each shot, they would review the picture, burst into peals of laughter, and then re-shoot, each new pose revealing an increasing desperation to show how happy and how in love they were.

If Curtis hadn't hassled me out of the apartment so quickly, I might have thought to bring my camera and got a shot or two of the Sagrada Família at night. And Curtis was right—it did look more impressive in the dark with the floodlighting and the black sky as a backdrop.

A few good shots would really explain what I was seeing as I looked at the Nativity façade with its four main spires of intricately carved yellowed stone that seemed to be melting. I didn't have the words to explain on my blog just how crazy the building looked, and yet how stunning it is.

But I hadn't thought to bring my camera, and while I was tempted to berate Curtis for our collective lack of foresight, I really didn't have the energy to try to get a rise out of him.

And last time I tried, it hadn't ended well for me.

Curtis squeezed my hand, drawing my attention back from the Sagrada Família. "Are you sure you're okay?"

"Mmm," I nodded, turning to see his head tilted as if demonstrating concern, but his eyes were flicking to take in the surroundings.

When he spoke again, he was hesitant. "Can I...have the...?" He pointed forward with his head as if that was sufficient explanation. When I didn't move, he continued, "The...envelope that..."

"Oh." I felt the embarrassed smile spread across my face as I finally understood. "Yeah, of course." I removed my left hand from on top of his and slipped it between the buttons of my blouse, singlehandedly manipulated the zip on the purse, and withdrew the envelope, holding it between two fingers as I offered it to Curtis.

Curtis had his thumb and forefinger pressed together as if holding a pinch of salt—he hesitated over whether to take the envelope he had just requested. "You're sure you're okay?" he asked again, his voice soft, reassuring.

I felt my head nodding.

"Really?" asked Curtis, lifting the envelope from my fingers.

A single nod.

Curtis stood. "I'll just be over here." He threw his head to the side. "I won't be out of sight. Okay?"

I shrugged.

He paused, looking intently at me.

"I'll be fine, Curtis."

He lingered a moment longer, then turned and started to limp away.

I first met Curtis in the tapas bar where I work. It's unusual for non-locals to come in, but it was great to hear a voice from home. He was only the second person from the States that I had chatted with since arriving in Barcelona. When I told him I was traveling and as part of that I was earning money working in the bar while trying to keep my expenses to a minimum, he offered me the room in his apartment.

Although calling it a room rather suggests that it is bigger than it is.

Or that there is any real storage space in the room.

But it is cheap.

Very cheap.

My room is actually the laundry room—there's a washing machine and a dryer in there. The passage in front of these is where Curtis slotted my bed—one side slammed up against the wall and the other with a gap of about six inches until I reach the machines. In other words, there's just enough space to walk through sideways. With the steel bedframe, my stuff then fits under the bed, and I can fit a few handfuls of clothes in the closet that also stores the apartment's bedding and towels, as well as all our cleaning supplies.

There are two other bedrooms: Curtis's room and the room that was occupied by Cooper Jones—our former resident Australian—before he moved out.

These were conventional rooms with space around the bed, closets without cleaning materials, a chest of drawers, and all the other things you associate with a bedroom, including rent. Curtis had made me a deal and sublet the laundry room for €50 a month.

I got somewhere clean to sleep for ten bucks a week and it was my room—no one was going to fight me for it. There was, of course, an exchange. In return for the cheap bed, I agreed to do the boys' laundry, keep the apartment tidy, and do a bit of what Curtis called *fetching and carrying* for him.

I didn't feel like I'd be upsetting the sisterhood by taking on the menial tasks. I had to do my own washing, plus I didn't want the boys in what was my room; I would vacuum pretty regularly anyway if I was there on my own. How much of an imposition was it to add a bit more to what I was already going to be doing? And it wasn't as if the guys created much washing—you don't when you wear the same jeans every day and only own two T-shirts, which was all Cooper seemed to own. And since they were out most of the time, most of the mess was mine.

I looked up at Curtis: He had reached two guys. There was some initial hesitation, like strangers meeting on a blind date, but as they began talking, the men started moving like wild animals sizing each other up before a fight.

These guys weren't local, but they weren't tourists either. At least, not regular tourists who always dress in a distinct way. The business tourists either dress to impress, knowing this is their one chance away from home, or if they've given up hope, they stay in the *smart-casual* clothes they have been wearing all day.

The tourists who come for pleasure always seem to buy a new wardrobe before they leave home and accessorize that with dual-function clothing—jackets with hundreds of pockets, hats with a compass built in, comfortable walking shoes marketed as being appropriate if you were asked to dinner with the ambassador...which were never comfortable after the first hour, nor were they smart.

And these two weren't part of the backpacker crowd, who were recognizable from their single set of footwear—usually sturdy boots—and their clothes that had been washed so often and in such bizarre ways that any color and texture had been scrubbed away, too.

Instead, these guys looked grubby: dirty jeans and a T-shirt under an olive military jacket for one, and a denim jacket for the other. Gray tennis shoes, and both had hair that was lank and uncut. The one is the denim jacket was twitching, looking around, while the other seemed completely focused on his conversation with Curtis. Or was that a negotiation with Curtis?

Curtis hadn't told me who they were, what was in the envelope he had taken back from me, or why we were here to meet them.

But then again, there were a lot of things that Curtis hadn't told me.

The final reason why I decided to accept Curtis's offer of a bed in the apartment was that it was close enough to the tapas bar for me to be able to walk home. It wasn't that I wanted to walk home at the end of the shift, but I could, and that would save me more money, meaning I could keep traveling for longer.

As I stayed in the apartment, I found Curtis becoming

more protective and thoughtful. He was like the brother I never had but every girl dreams of. That wasn't to say I trusted him beyond the confines of our apartment—I still didn't know how he had gotten the limp or the circumstances of him leaving the US Army. To be frank, I'd never seen any proof that he'd been in the army—it's not like he's a photos-on-the-mantelpiece type guy. More importantly, I didn't know how he was earning a living in Barcelona.

But what I did know was that I felt safe in the apartment. He was respectful—he knocked on my door, even though it was never shut, and he never *accidentally* walked in on me in the shower. I never came home to find my underwear rearranged.

As well as making me feel safe inside the apartment, Curtis was keen to make sure I knew how to protect myself outside. He taught me how to take control of a situation by bending fingers back, as I had when the groping started. As he told me, it's not a perfect solution, but it makes your position clear and is less aggressive than other options, which means you can stop a situation from escalating.

But if de-escalation didn't work and I was still in danger, then Curtis's solution was simple: hit them. Hit them and make it count. If you were going to resort to violence, then there was no point in underplaying a hand—the only solution was to make a definitive show of force.

When it came to a definitive show of force, Curtis offered two options. The first: a kick or, preferably, a knee applied to the testicles with maximum aggression. He reassured me that as long as I connected, then the application of sufficient force would cause enough pain to incapacitate the guy so I could make my getaway, assuming there was only one guy. I liked the idea, but there was no way I could have applied it in practice tonight, when surrounded by the drummers and the guys chanting. I could have taken one down, but the rest would have still been there.

The second option: the knee. Curtis said that the fastest way to debilitate someone was to hit the knee from the side—you can do horrible, possibly permanent damage and hurt the person a lot, but be sure you wouldn't kill them.

Maybe making sure I knew how to look after myself made Curtis feel calmer when he sent me out on my fetch-and-carry missions. Curtis had me dropping packages off—usually small packages, about the size of a paperback book, sometimes smaller than that, around the size of an envelope with a very long letter. It wasn't a problem for me—I was earning my cheap rent and saving Curtis from putting too much stress on his injured leg.

Sometimes, like tonight, Curtis wanted me to go some-where with him. He never explained why he wanted me, and he never took me anywhere that made me feel unsafe, but it was part of the deal, and it would mean that when, in a few months, I decided to move on from Barcelona, I would have a bigger stack of money in the bank account.

Curtis and the smaller of the two guys shook hands and simultaneously rocked forward, bumping their shoulder together. At this point I would normally expect to see the free hand come around and slap the other guy on the back.

At least, that's what usually happens in the movies.

But not here. Instead, it seemed like the two left hands, like the right hands, were between the bodies as they touched. But it was quick, the three guys were at a distance, it was dark, and I hadn't been paying that much attention.

Curtis twisted his body, his head remaining facing the guys as they said a few last words. He took his first steps, reached down to his jeans and slipped a hand into the front-right pocket. His head flicked toward me, his look hawk-like. Accusing, questioning, ready to attack.

He looked back to the other two, said something, then started to walk briskly toward me. As he walked he slapped his pockets, then plunged his hands into his pockets. With each step closer, his stare became more accusing.

"The fuckers," he said. "The fuckers got me. I'm gonna..." He voice was quiet, but the tone dripped acid.

"Those guys? What have they done?" I asked. "And who

were they, anyway?"

"Not them." Apparently, from his tone, it was obvious. "Those fucking drummers." He exhaled loudly and sat. "This wasn't about you—this was about me. Well, it was about you—but it was also about me."

He seemed to sense the confusion that I was sure my face conveyed. "They pushed you until I reacted. And when I flipped, they grabbed my wallet." He paused. "Don't you see? They felt you up to find what you were carrying, then when I wouldn't do that bloody high five shit—which they only do to make tourists lift their hands out of their pockets—they started hassling you until I reacted, and when I reacted..."

"They took your wallet," I finished. "Why didn't you give me the wallet? That third-boob look might catch on."

It was Curtis's turn to look confused.

"What was in the wallet anyway?"

"Cash. Quite a lot. Our address..." His voice faded. When he continued, his tone was soft but resolute. "Other stuff... We've gotta get it back."

I looked up at him, hoping my stare was questioning.

"Now," he said. "We've gotta get it back now."

three

The sound of the drums was familiar as it broke through the bustle of the night. The beat of the rhythm was as hypnotic as it had been when we last saw them.

"See," said Curtis. "I told you this was where they would be heading. This is their happy hunting ground: Look at all the tourists."

"Look at all the drunk tourists," I muttered, checking my phone; it was just past 10 PM.

It had taken us nearly an hour to track down the group at the top of La Rambla, the near mile-long street that started at Plaça de Catalunya, a large square often regarded as the city center and the place where the old city and the 19th century–built city meet. The five streets making up La Rambla then lead between the Gothic Quarter and what was loosely the Chinatown area of Barcelona, eventually finding their way to the port. The port where tourists migrate during the evening to the bars and nightclubs, and the prostitutes.

The trail had started at the place where we originally encountered the musicians—a nondescript five-way junction that seemed to be something of a crossing point, making it unusually busy. I held Curtis's arm tightly as we paused at the scene. From there, we followed what we expected to be their track: At each intersection where we had a choice of options, we followed the road with more people. And if two roads seemed to have broadly equal numbers of people, we took the one that seemed to have the greater number of tourists.

Either the strategy was good or we were lucky, and we caught sight of them while they were still crossing Plaça de Catalunya Square, just north of La Rambla. We would have stopped moving sooner, but when we got our first glance Curtis decided we should dive around the backstreets and get in front of the musicians so we could watch as they worked their trade along the tourist-trap street.

As the group of musicians moved, the guy in blue orbited, making his animal noises. He made the sound of a kooka-burra. "Look," said Curtis, nodding toward the man. "That's the sound he made when he saw us—I bet he's just seen some fresh meat."

The black Jesus-like character had heard the signal and seemed to be looking in the same direction as the blue-suited spotter, looking for the pack's prey.

"They're American, aren't they?" I said with little enthu-siasm as I looked at a husband and wife who, from the way they presented themselves—him in a brown-checkered jacket, her in a puce nylon jacket, both in manmade fabric slacks that were far too tight and sneakers that no teenager would ever wear, with a large camera around the husband's neck—could only be our fellow countrymen. "We should save them, Curtis."

"Can't," he whispered. "If we go in, then they'll know we've seen them. We need surprise."

The guy in white was in front of the husband—his arms outstretched as if being pulled on a cross, his head thrown back as he chanted with the others following his lead. The wife was swinging her ass, unfortunately not in time with the beat of the drums. Jesus held up his hand—the husband accepted the high five. The guy in red moved up by the wife and playfully bumped his ass into hers.

"Bastard." I heard myself say.

The guy in the green-and-orange-checkered robe had moved in behind the husband as Jesus held up his hand for another high five. "See that?" asked Curtis.

"See what?"

"Mister Green and Orange just got his wallet and some-thing from one of her pockets. Both within five seconds and neither noticed—they just think they're being bumped as the guys dance close."

"But..." I didn't know what to say as I continued

watching, seeing the group of kids swarm through the group of musicians and two tourists.

Curtis sighed. It was almost a sigh of admiration. "That's why!"

"What's why?" I asked.

"The kids." His voice still had a tone of admiration, but there was regret. "Mister Green and Orange handed off the pickings to the kids. That means the cops have got about fifteen seconds to catch the guys with whatever they've grabbed, and after that, the evidence is gone."

I tried to look, but the kids were all running away from the musicians surrounding the American tourists. The guy in blue had left the group but was still screeching and making animal noises as he proceeded in the direction of the port. The kids all came together—now that they moved as one I could see that there were four of them—and ran in the opposite direction.

About fifty yards away, there were two women. Normally, these two women would blend into the background and be totally unnoticeable—their dark skin would help them to become invisible in the darkness. But these two immediately caught my attention. For a start, they were both totally focused on the kids—it was like they had radar tracking forcing their eyeballs to remain focused on the kids even when they were hidden from direct sight.

And then there was how they dressed.

Or at least how the one standing on the left was dressed. The one on the right wore jeans, a white T-shirt, and a black jacket, probably leather. The one of the left was dressed in a robe that reached the ground, with long sleeves. Diagonal stripes alternated between a thinner faded olive green stripe and a thicker-patterned stripe, which was a skewed yellow diamond surrounded by a broad red border and with blue piping between each diamond. Her hair was held up by a scarf fashioned from the same material and tied with a large bow on the top—but slightly to the right—of her head.

As the kids neared, the tension in the women's faces

relaxed and broad smiles broke out. The woman in jeans squatted to greet the kids, and the one in the African dress leaned forward.

Everything the kids were carrying was given to the two women, whose attention immediately focused on the haul. With the kids swarming in front of the women, it was hard to see what they were doing, but as they both stood upright, the woman in jeans seemed to be stuffing her pockets while the other was holding something. The woman in African dress clumsily passed the items she was clutching to the other, who held the bundle equally clumsily as she turned away and started walking from the group.

A short way up the street she passed a trashcan, and without breaking step she dumped her load before continuing to walk away. Pulling my gaze back to the other woman, she remained with the kids, clucking around like a mother hen proud of her chicks' work.

"They're good," said Curtis, unable to keep the admiration out of his voice. "Very, very good. They work like a machine...a piece of precision engineering. A Swiss watch of thievery."

I grunted. "What?"

"Look!" He threw a hand in the direction of the musicians. "The guy in blue. He's the fisherman—he catches the punters and reels them in, leaving the guy in white to take them off the hook. Once they're there, then Blue Suit is on crowd control—he diverts attention so no one sees what's happening, and he's on the outside, acting as the lookout for trouble. Any cops, and he's bound to have a sound that means nothing to us but means everything to the others."

Curtis was right. The musicians were moving slowly down the street, dancing and chanting as they went. The guy in blue was twenty or thirty yards ahead of them and was making a chirruping sound. At the same time, his arm was raised and his hand pointing. Everyone else would have seen an African guy dancing, but as I stood there, I could see him pointing at the next potential targets. I flicked my eyes back to the black Jesus-like character in white. My suspicion was right: The target had been identified, and Black Jesus was moving the drummers toward them.

"Now look at the guy in red," said Curtis as we watched the swarm subsume their next victims. "He's all buddy-buddy and in a nonthreatening way; by bumping asses he's getting them used to being touched. And that's the thing—the victims need to feel that being touched is normal. Once they feel it's normal, then they won't flinch or react when the hands go into their pockets."

The Jesus-character—his arms spread wide as he called to the heavens—moved in. "And now begins the religious experience—a guy in white looking like he's been strapped to a crucifix. Notice how he makes them feel that it's a religious experience and it's all about them." He paused, watching. "Now watch—here it comes." Jesus raised his hands and high fived one of his new victims. "And now look at the green and orange—he's got his hands through their pockets."

There was a cry from Jesus—a heart-rending sob to the heavens. Curtis smiled. "That was the signal."

"What signal?"

"The kids." Curtis was right—the kids swarmed into the group, ducking through, circling, jumping, shouting, laughing, and then simultaneously they were returning. Like mercury turned from individual blobs to a single lump, moving as one to the mother hen.

"Where's the other woman?" I asked. "The one with jeans and the jacket."

"Dumping the wallets and storing the cash." He looked toward me. "Getting rid of the evidence and banking their earnings...although I doubt they go near many banks."

I was getting uncomfortable watching people be robbed in the street and I was ready for bed, but since I still felt some level of responsibility for getting Curtis's wallet stolen, I needed to offer some practical assistance. "Let's go back and find your wallet—we might not get your cash, but we can get what they've left and then go home. We found them: We know where they took your wallet, we know the route they followed, so it can't be that hard to find the trashcan where your wallet was dumped."

It seemed simple to me.

It seemed like the swiftest way to end the evening and get home.

Curtis shook his head. The twist in his lips suggested he didn't want to disappoint me. When he started talking, he was hesitant. "I'm not going..." He paused as if trying to order his thoughts; when he continued, his tone was dismissive. "That'll take far too long, and if we don't find the wallet, then they'll be gone by the time we get back here."

"Then you follow them and I'll go and look."

"Look where?" There was annoyance in his tone. "Look where precisely? The route we followed and every side street from the route? How far do you go up each side street—five minutes, the first three trashcans?" He sighed, trying to be more diplomatic. "I'm sorry, it's not practical. I just need to ask them directly...and get my money back."

I went to speak but stopped when I locked eyes with Curtis. There was anger there. He wasn't angry at me, but the testosterone was flowing, and he was readying himself for an argument. He softened again. "There are lots of them, so I'm not intending a big fight, but I do need to talk." His eyes locked more firmly on mine. "This is what I'm going to do."

As he explained, it seemed quite reasonable, and all I needed to do was keep watch. I figured five or ten minutes, then we'd be on our way home.

four

I was hazy on the detailed mechanics of Curtis's plan, but it didn't seem to be much more complicated than waiting until the group was in the middle of robbing someone and walking up for a chat.

But first we had to wait until there were fewer people around. Curtis assured me he wasn't going to throw a punch, but if he needed to defend himself, then he wanted fewer witnesses—and he didn't want any have-a-go heroes coming to defend the musicians.

Fewer people, but there had to be some people—or victims, as I called them, much to Curtis's chagrin—so that we could step in.

While the mechanics were hazy, my role was simple: I would stand a few steps back from Curtis. "Are you ready?" he asked.

The simple response to the question was no. "No, I'm not ready, and I never will be." Suddenly I had become aware of my heart pounding, and that my mouth was dry, which seemingly rendered me mute.

"Okay. Quietly," said Curtis, taking my silence as affirmation as we moved toward the group. "Drop back," he whispered and I slowed, licking my lips to try to get some moisture around my mouth.

The woman in the jeans and jacket had left about three minutes earlier. Last time she left she was gone for around fifteen minutes—hopefully she would be gone for a similar length this time. The woman in African dress flicked an anxious glance at Curtis as he walked past her and then returned her fixated stare to the kids, who were running between the drummers.

I held back, stopping behind the den mother's field of vision as Curtis continued toward the group. The rhythm pounded, asses were being bumped, Jesus was calling to the heavens, and the guy in the green-and-orange-checkered robe was stepping back while the guy in the royal-blue suit was making a loud clicking sound.

I could hear the kids' laughter: This was a game to them. They didn't realize they were members of a modern-day Dickensian street gang. The kids filtered out from the circle, and the den mother took a step forward, the tension in her shoulders visibly relaxing.

The swarm of kids mingled into a single mass heading past Curtis and toward the den mother, who leaned forward, lowering her head toward the height of their eye line.

As the mass of kids passed Curtis, he shot out an arm. There was a yelp from one of the kids as he was pulled toward Curtis. The den mother let out a small shriek and returned to the upright, unsure of what had just happened.

Curtis gripped the kid tightly. The plan had been hazy, but I wasn't about to get involved in child kidnapping.

The den mother, with the remaining kids now clinging to her, called out—I didn't understand the language and couldn't figure out who she was talking to.

"Police," I said. She spun to face me. I tugged at the edge of my jacket as if showing her a badge. I wasn't sure what to say, but I hoped she had seen the same TV shows that I had and that she was assuming I had just shown her my badge.

I fixed my stare on her, then pointed with my head, away from Curtis. She took the hint and pulled the children close, hastily hustling them away, but shouting something over her shoulder as she went.

Whatever she said, it caught Jesus's attention. He stood facing Curtis, silent and without calling for help from above. One drummer had stopped playing, but the bigger drummer—the guy with the serious face—continued playing a simple rhythm on his deep drum. The ass bumper in the red robe put his arm around the two victims, who had yet to learn that they were victims, and quietly led them in the other direction.

The kid began to whimper. Curtis pulled him closer, and there was a muffled cry.

"He's a kid, Curtis," I hissed. No reaction. "Curtis!" Still no reaction.

Jesus in his white robe took a step toward Curtis. He looked weary, but he had probably been impressing tourists for the last two hours—it was hard physical labor to keep up an act like that. His gaze seemed fixed on the kid that Curtis was holding in an arm lock.

Curtis shrugged at Jesus, then indicated the kid. It was as if he was suggesting a trade.

Jesus said nothing—he just continued to stare at the kid. I didn't see what Curtis did, but the kid let out yell. Jesus took another step forward, holding his arms out at waist height. He said something to Curtis, and Curtis made a single shake of his head and then pulled the kid tighter.

I took a few steps, walking the circumference of a quarter-circle with Curtis and the kid in the middle, in an attempt to catch Curtis's eye. He didn't react, but from my new vantage point I could see a trail of liquid in front of the kid, flowing down the slight incline of the street. "For fuck's sake, Curtis," I hissed and was rewarded with a flash of a stare, his eyes like someone was forcing them open in a laboratory experiment.

Jesus muttered something—I wasn't sure whether I hadn't heard properly or it was a foreign language—as he moved forward, his hands held in an "I surrender" pose.

Curtis muttered a retort. Jesus might have heard, but I couldn't. However, Jesus was clearly unfazed and took another step toward Curtis, the tips of his fingers now touching his head, tears forming in his eyes.

And then time stood still. In a single move, Curtis released the kid and he was gone, sprinting to find his friends and the den mother, who had all disappeared. Before I was aware the kid was moving—before Jesus was able to think beyond his relief that the kid was moving—Curtis had loaded his right fist and landed a blow in the white-robed man's solar plexus.

I heard the air being expelled from his lungs, rushing like the wind coming off the ocean as he bent forward.

Curtis was ready for this reaction and grabbed the other man's head, pulling it down as he raised his knee. I'm sure I could hear the cartilage and bones give way as the nose and knee made contact. Curtis didn't release; instead, he pulled the other man to an upright position admiring his work as the blood flowed over the white robe.

Behind the blood, I couldn't tell whether Jesus had more damage than a cracked nose. I wondered whether his cheekbone was damaged too, but I didn't have a clear enough idea of how it looked before his face met the force of Curtis's knee. What I did know was that he was struggling to stay upright; he had thrown a leg back and was holding his arm back seemingly to keep his balance.

The guy with the green-and-orange-checkered robe was moving up behind Jesus, who was waving his arm behind him, trying to balance.

"Back." I heard Curtis. The checkered robe didn't move—if anything, he went closer to Jesus. "Back!" shouted Curtis, and the third man moved away.

A flash of light reflected off a streetlight. I let out a scream—Curtis looked to me instead of looking to the knife that I had seen reflected in the streetlight and that was now in Jesus's hand. He realized his mistake as Jesus made contact with him.

As Jesus pulled the knife back there was fresh blood on the blade.

Curtis loosed his hand closest to me and made contact with the man with the knife. The blow didn't have the effect of his first punch, and the man in the bloody white robe staggered toward Curtis, waving the knife in the air. With his limp, Curtis couldn't move backwards quickly, but he could sway from side to side with some speed. That didn't seem to stop Jesus from making some contact with him two or three times as he slashed.

The two men stood facing each other, breathing heavily.

I saw the edge of Curtis's mouth twitch as he raised his left hand. He snapped his fingers and pointed over the other man's shoulder. With some sort of involuntary motion, Jesus began turning his head to look where Curtis had pointed, slowing as he realized that Curtis had pushed his left shoulder forward to draw his right back. And when his shoulder was fully drawn, Curtis released his fist, stepping forward to bring his full body weight behind the punch.

The fist made contact with the upper arm, and Jesus dropped the knife—there was a muted clang as it hit the ground. Jesus reached for the knife, throwing his left leg toward the blade. As one leg moved, the other—where he kept his foot stationary—leaned diagonally.

Curtis moved away from the blade, and as Jesus reached for the knife Curtis projected his full weight on the diagonally stretched leg, stamping down on the outside of the other man's knee. Jesus screamed as he fell to the ground, reaching for the blade. Curtis fell on him, moving the blade out of his reach, and landed three swift blows to his face, knocking the other man's head against the solid ground.

"Enough!" I said, surprised at how calm my voice was.

The guy in the green and orange robe stepped toward his comrade. Curtis reached for the blade and pointed it toward him, waiting until the man stepped back; as he did Curtis returned his attention to the bloody white-robed mess in front of him. He looked him over as if assessing the damage and then tugged at the white robe around the fallen man's waist.

He took the knife and looked down at the taut fabric. The ass bumper in red shouted something, his tone pleading. Curtis looked up and smiled before returning his attention to the fabric and cutting a large square of white material.

He stood, knife in one hand and cloth in the other. "Come on, Monty. Let's get going."

five

The knife went down the first storm drain we passed. "I only took it so they didn't use it," said Curtis, his voice weak, his movements strained.

That was the last he said for a while as we continued slowly down La Rambla, his limp more pronounced. We headed in the direction of the port along the broad sweep of the pedestrianized core with its wavy brickwork, flanked by narrow roads on either side where black and yellow taxis shifted tourists at speed and mopeds fizzed along. The roads were held in by the tall buildings on either side—a mixture of old, where each window had a wrought-iron balcony, and faceless new. Each new building seeming to house a bank or another financial institution.

We continued past the street kiosks set like mousetraps to catch unwary tourists, until we reached a row of tables and chairs with umbrellas, opposite a McDonald's.

Curtis pulled out one of the metal seats. It wasn't that he actively sat—it was more that his muscles seemed to all give way simultaneously, and he dropped on the seat like a big, shapeless dollop of cream being dropped on the floor. This was the first time that I had looked him in the face since we left the Jesus-like figure inert on the ground, with his people coming to surround him in the hope of resurrection.

I was still trying to process my revulsion at Curtis taking a kid hostage as I looked down at him in the chair. In the dark, with only a few streetlights and restaurants to provide illumination, the mid-brown toned skin on Curtis's arm looked black. It took me a few moments to realize that the liquid black smeared over his arm was blood.

I heard myself gasp like a helpless girl in a 1950s movie. "Curtis!" Three passing businesspeople—two women and one man—looked at me, then decided they didn't want to be involved and casually looked past me, as if they were surveying a historic monument in the distance. If I hadn't known they were staring at McDonald's, I might've had more respect.

I pulled up a chair and sat facing Curtis, looking at his arm. The cut was maybe six inches long, crossing his arm diagonally. It looked bad—blood still seemed to be flowing—but I couldn't see how deep the cut was, not that I know what's good or bad in terms of depth of a knife wound.

The chill of the breeze being funneled directly from the Mediterranean was becoming uncomfortably cold for me, and I had a jacket on. Curtis only had a T-shirt but didn't seem to notice the temperature. "You should go to hospital. Get someone to look at that. Maybe get a stitch or two."

Slowly he turned his head to look down at his arm, then sighed. "It just needs to be cleaned up." His left hand moved to his injury, the square of cloth between his fingers. When he'd cut the fabric it appeared to be white—now he was awkwardly turning the material with one hand, searching for an unbloodied patch.

He tilted his head up as he moved the fabric to his arm. "See. It just needs to be cleaned."

I looked closer. "It needs to be cleaned and stitched. That's a long gash." He had the look that said he knew I was right, but that he wasn't going to admit it. At least not right now. "Shall I get some water to rinse your wound?" I tilted my head back, in the direction of McDonald's.

"Yeah," he mouthed as he dabbed at his arm.

I stood slowly, looking past his arm. His T-shirt had cuts that hadn't been there when we left the apartment, and behind these slashes, there were blood trails—one about the size of a fist, one a quarter that size, and the third smaller, but it had flowed down his shirt, becoming a series of drips just before the small river reached the hem.

I thought about the crumpled heap we'd left on the street. The musicians were probably less than a quarter of a mile away—within earshot if they were playing their drums—but

I could hear nothing. More significantly, I could see nothing: There were no colorful robes, no darting characters. All I could see were tourists, darkness, and the tables from empty pavement cafés. All I could hear was the hum of traffic, a few shouts of drunk tourists, and the occasional low electronic beat as a bar door opened.

"I'll be back as soon..." As soon as what? "I'll...get your water." Curtis lifted his eyes to acknowledge me, and I turned to jog over to McDonald's, checking that I could feel the emergency bill I kept in my purse.

The water was chilled and came in half-liter bottles. I got six and carried them over to Curtis, putting them on the table and opening the first. "Hold your arm still," I said as I let the water flow over into the wound to flush through the laceration. As the water washed the injury, I sat, feeling the change from the €50 bill in my back pocket.

"I didn't feel the cut...the cuts." Curtis was mumbling. "I knew he had a blade—well, I knew he had a blade when I felt it. But I didn't realize it was the knife doing damage. I do now...and it hurts."

His voice lacked strength. I wasn't sure whether it was a result of his injury or if he was conserving his energy. On two occasions I'd seen him after he got in some sort of a scrap, but I'd never seen him after this sort of injury.

I finished the first bottle and opened the second. "Do you want a sip before I start pouring?"

Curtis nodded. I handed him the bottle and looked closer. "That's a clean cut, Curtis. You need it stitched."

"Keep rinsing it," he said, passing back the water, "and then tie this around it." He placed the bloody square of cloth on the arm of my chair. I finished tipping the second bottle, then opened the third and tried to rinse out the cloth.

"How much blood have you lost?" I asked.

Curtis reached forward with his uninjured arm, gesturing toward the bottle. I passed it so he could take another sip. He held the bottle up, looking at the contents, then momentarily tipped it, immediately righting it. A splash of water hit the ground, spraying in all directions.

Curtis looked back at the bottle. "See that—a few drops of water, but it looks like I dropped a bucket of water." I frowned slightly, not really able to see much in the dark. "It looks worse than it is—a little blood goes a long way."

"That's not a little blood," I said, wringing out the cloth and taking the water back to douse the fabric some more. I wrung the cloth for a second time, then opened it up before folding it to make a strip. "It's not that clean, but bring your arm over here."

Curtis raised his arm as I leaned forward to put the makeshift bandage around it. "You're going to have to tie it tight," he said. I crossed the fabric, seating the knot inside his arm and away from the wound, and pulled tight.

"Maximize the pressure to stop the last bleeding," said Curtis.

"So we *are* agreed that this is a serious wound," I said, putting a second knot on top of the first to stop the bandage from slipping. Curtis didn't reply. "You need stitches—you need a hospital."

"I need a drink," said Curtis, his voice displaying more strength than it had since he got stabbed. "In fact, I need several drinks. The cut's not deep—that bit of cloth should pull the skin together, and a few shots will ease the pain."

I looked at the bandage—it wasn't doing anything more than acting as a bit of decoration on Curtis's arm. I gently pulled the lower edge. It slipped. "You need something better than that. I'll be right back."

I dashed to the nearest tourist kiosk, found a shadow on the sheltered side, and stood facing in. A quick look—to the left, then the right—no one was coming. I unbuttoned my blouse—checked left and right again—then slipped off my jacket, took off my blouse and held it between my teeth, and put on my jacket again, buttoning it fully. I stood out of the shadow and checked my look in a window and glanced down to make sure I wasn't misbuttoned.

Curtis had a quizzical expression. "Let's do your arm

properly," I said.

He shrugged and offered his slipped bandage, which I removed from his arm and rinsed through with water before wringing it out and folding it into a square. "Dressing," I said, holding the square, "and this should keep it in place." I held up my blouse. "But I'm warning you, Curtis Washington: If you bleed on my blouse, then you will be in deeper shit than you are already."

If he wanted alcohol, then he was ready to be told how stupid he had been and how he had put us both at risk for no gain.

"What am I in the shit for now?" asked Curtis as I rolled my blouse.

I picked up the dressing and pointed to his arm—he held it out. I slapped the dressing on the wound, hard. "Ow!" I wasn't sure whether it was the shock or actual pain that caused Curtis to react. "That hurts."

"Now think how that kid felt, Curtis."

He sighed. It was the sound of exasperation. "I needed to get the guy to come to me—he wouldn't come if I asked. I only grabbed the kid to get their attention. I didn't hurt the kid."

"Didn't hurt the kid?" I looked down at his hands splayed across his knees as he leaned forward to push his arm out so I could apply the dressing. Even in the gloom I could see his knuckles glowing like a prizefighter's. The knuckles on his right hand looked to be throbbing more than those on the left hand. As he stared intently at me, I rapped my knuckles on his. I knew it would hurt me.

"Ow!" he said. "Ow again!" It hurt me, but it hurt him more.

"You didn't hurt the kid, you say?"

"Are you tending to his wounds?" Curtis was indignant.

"Curtis, the kid pissed himself. You said we were going to get your wallet back—not that we were going to kidnap a kid. Not that you were going to hurt a kid—and you *did* hurt him. Didn't you hear him whimper?"

Curtis remained silent. The anger in his eyes seemed to be quelling.

"And we didn't get your wallet back. Not that you seemed to ask for it."

Curtis was still quiet. I knew he wasn't able to meet my stare, so I started to wrap my blouse around the square bandage on his arm. On the third wrap I tied the first knot, pulling it tight as I continued speaking. "Let me summarize. In the last thirty minutes, you've kidnapped a kid, you've hurt yourself in a fight, you haven't found your wallet, and you stand no chance of getting your wallet back—unless some Good Samaritan happens to see our address inside. In other words, all you've done is make our situation worse, and you won't go to the hospital, but instead you want alcohol."

six

Apparently the treatment for stabbing is shots.

Tequila shots.

And none of that salt and lime business—just the shots, straight and in quick succession.

My limit was three, but I hadn't been stabbed. I was also drinking on an empty stomach, so after the shots I had a beer—just one—then, remembering I had to work tomorrow, I switched to coffee. After the second coffee, I stopped—I wanted to stand a chance of sleeping.

Curtis, however, kept on with the shots while I was on the beer, only stopping when I got my coffee. He tried to claim that he was only ordering more shots to stay in favor with the barman, who had been kind and let us use the first-aid kit. I felt happier with a proper dressing on the wound but was rather distressed with the state of my blouse, which was now tied around my waist.

The alcohol numbed Curtis's pain and helped to calm me, giving me that feeling I get after drinking. It was more of a disconnectedness: When I turned my head, it felt like my brain took a while to catch up with the movement and my eyes had trouble finding what I was trying to look at.

I still thought Curtis was wrong to grab the kid, and I worried about the damage he had done to the guy in the white robe. That said, I did see firsthand how effective a well-aimed kick to the side of the knee can be—after Curtis landed on the knee, the guy went down and didn't get up again.

It was past midnight. "How are we getting home?" I asked.

"Youssef," was his single-word response. Youssef was a skinny Moroccan guy with a wispy beard who worked as a cab driver, although from one or two things Curtis had said,

I inferred that he might from time to time transport more than drunk tourists.

The first time I met Youssef was about ten days after I moved into the apartment. He had been attacked in his cab.

Curtis bought him back to the apartment. He was quite a mess, but after he cleaned up, his wounds didn't look as bad as they first had. He was still badly shaken and didn't want to say anything other than some passengers had started arguing with him.

While I was doing the tending-the-sick thing, Curtis disappeared. I chatted with Youssef for a while, and it became obvious that he was in no condition to go out, so I put him to bed in the only bed that I knew could be free—mine. He fell asleep virtually immediately, and I went out and looked at his cab. Whoever had beaten him had beaten his cab too, paying particular attention to the side mirrors, which were hanging off the doors.

That was potentially an expensive job—the mirrors aren't just glass, there are the plastic shells holding the electrics to move the mirrors and the built-in turn signals. Take the car to a main dealer, and they'll replace the whole unit, which costs hundreds of Euros—and twice that for Youssef, since both mirrors were hanging off. Plus labor charges.

I made a quick guess and figured Youssef would be paying around €1,500.

A mechanic had a workshop around the corner—I'd only seen him once, but I figured it was worth a chance. I parked the cab across his front entrance and posted the keys with my number. Then I went home and slept, badly, on the sofa.

It was far too early when the phone rang. I said "cinco minutos," and I was there in five minutes. The mechanic was short, pot-bellied, wearing greasy overalls, and with greasy hands—everything you expect a mechanic to be. He also only spoke Spanish. But he did understand the problem—not that it was difficult to comprehend.

He pointed to his wrist—where people used to wear watches—and said "dos horas." Even with my limited

Spanish, I knew that was two hours. I pulled out some cash and held it front of him—then shrugged, considering the question. "Ciento," he replied.

I nodded, shook his hand, and said, "Dos horas." Then I went to find some breakfast for Youssef, all the while looking for something to wipe the grime off my hand.

When he woke, Youssef seemed to think I'd got the deal of the year. I thought I was just doing what was necessary to help him keep earning money.

Curtis called from my phone, and Youssef's black and yellow Toyota was outside waiting for us within three minutes, ready to swiftly thread its way back to our apartment.

Our street wasn't on the tourist trail. For a start, it was narrow: one car-width narrow, with steel posts sunk into the edge of the sidewalks to reinforce the message that there was only room for one car—no bumping up on the curb. There were similarities between the buildings, but each was different—some were brick-faced, others rendered, usually in cement. Most had balconies, and all were set over at least four floors. Where there were balconies on each side of the street—particularly where the higher balconies projected farther across the street—the effect was of a tunnel.

At street level there were some businesses—hair salons, a family café, a copy and office services shop—but at this time of night, they were shuttered. Most of the metals shutters had a light covering of graffiti. Where there were private residences on the ground level, these all had sturdy iron bars covering the windows.

Although the buildings were comparatively new, electricity seemed to have been an afterthought. Telephones and satellite TV were an even later thought. Cabling ran over all the outside walls—ugly black junction boxes spewing spider webs of cables across the fronts and up and down every building, and about every twenty or thirty yards, a cable stretched across the road. Some cables across the road went directly—as if someone had planned the cable that way—but most went at an odd angle, often changing floors.

"Slow it," said Curtis. I looked forward to see what he was looking at. In the distance there was a blue flashing light. We crossed a junction heading toward the light. "Shit," he muttered. "Pull up at the next junction."

"I…"

"Shh. I know," said Curtis.

"So are they after you for the kid or did you kill that guy? If you'd actually tried to get your wallet back, we…" Curtis spun to face me. Somehow it felt less necessary at that moment to continue to lecture him on his mistakes. "What are we going to do, Curtis?"

The side of his mouth twitched, pushing out his cheek. Finally he spoke. "I can't. But they've got nothing on you… You go in, and I'll…I dunno, I'll do something."

I sat in the back seat, gripping my bloodied blouse, staring at Curtis. Youssef turned to face me, offering no words.

"You want me to walk up to the cops with a bloody blouse?"

Curtis half shrugged. "It's my blood. Why shouldn't you have my blood your blouse?" I felt myself deflating as Curtis reached for the door, pushing it open. "You'll be fine—you need your sleep, you said so yourself."

As we had walked from the bar to the cab, I had thought I was holding Curtis up. Now that I was standing on my own, it seemed that actually he had been holding me. Or was I just shivering? Curtis gave a mock half-salute as Youssef turned right and drifted away. My last sight was the taillights, the only sound was the soft hiss of tires on blacktop.

I've never felt unsafe in our street, but it makes me nervous. At the street level, the steel superstructure holding the upper floors is rendered in cement, giving regular pillars and setback entrances. A couple finding themselves overtaken by their emotions may be harmless, but the sounds they make—when hidden in a dark corner—can be menacing. And after a few drinks, my mind tends to run a bit wilder.

Ironically, as I got closer to the police car and the small crowd that had gathered, I felt safer and more anonymous. I was now the one in the shadows.

The police car had pulled up outside the next block and was awkwardly angled between two steel posts, blocking both the street and the pedestrian sidewalk. I kept my eyes down and slipped through the door into our block.

"It was the Duchess," hissed Ana, the sound bouncing off the tiled floor of the entrance hall. I hadn't noticed her front door was ajar, but now it was swinging open as she continued talking. "You know, the old woman who says she's related to that crazy Countess who's always marrying her driver or her dance partner or some other young, fit dude."

I stood uncomfortably with my hands holding my blouse behind my back and leaned against the side of her door, trying to ignore her black satin nightdress with red detailing, which was both too short and too revealingly transparent.

"She was burgled."

I made an "oh" shape with my mouth. I was sorry that an old lady had been burgled, but I didn't care. I couldn't picture who she was, and I didn't want to listen to Ana—I knew where the conversation would go, and I had a bloody blouse that I needed to clean.

A grin spread across her face. "I wouldn't normally, but you know..." "You know" was Ana's way of saying there were men in uniform—in this case, the two police officers I had seen as I slipped in. She had a need to be worshipped by men and something of a near fetish for men in uniform. "But they weren't..." Which was her way of saying that these guys were probably in their fifties and, unsurprisingly for government employees, didn't appear to have several million Euros to lavish on her. "Did he take you anywhere nice?"

I shrugged. She had asked the question, but that was only to deflect her own disappointment and probably a realization that chasing any police car down your own street is not the road to happiness.

"The fact that you're home and not at his place tells me

everything I need to know, so I hope you at least had a good meal." Unlike her, I didn't sleep with guys on a first date or sometimes before a first date.

"I started drinking to blot out the pain," I said, not wanting to tell her I'd been out with Curtis.

"I've been there," she said. "I have been there." The words "been" and "there" were articulated with a weight that suggested a religious significance. In truth, however, all she meant was she had been on a lot of bad dates, which was an unfortunate side effect of being indiscriminate about who she dated and being so insecure that she needed to go out every night for men to prove they were attracted to her—and when she happened to be in, she still found a way to chase random strangers in uniform.

"I should be..." I said.

"Yeah, I need to... We should hit the town again sometime. Double trouble on the loose."

"We should," I said, remembering that when we last went out, I swore to myself that we would never go out again. "I'll catch you later." I turned, was halfway up the stairs when I heard her door close, and was in my front door before any other neighbor could see me.

The apartment felt empty. Partly that was because it *was* empty: There really wasn't that much stuff. But also, it was the tiled floors and the unadorned plaster walls without much in the way of soft furnishings to soak up the sound reflections.

The beige emulsion on the walls always took on a gray hue under the low-energy bulbs. Not an unpleasant gray—heck, if there was such a thing as *warm gray*, this was it—but it did look gray.

I went straight to the kitchen, pulled out a bucket from under the sink, and started to fill it as I grabbed the tub of prewash powder from on top of the dryer in my room. Returning to the kitchen, I dropped two scoops of powder into the filling bucket, and swirled the mix before dropping my blouse in.

I looked down: There was blood on my jeans—that would stain, too. Someone once told me that white clothes used to be washed with blue ink to make the white seem whiter. If this was true and my jeans did run, then hopefully it would counteract the mess made of my blouse by Curtis's blood.

It was too late to think any further, so I slipped off my jeans, emptied the pockets, and pushed the blue fabric into the bucket with the blouse.

I walked out of the kitchen, past the front door, and paused, looking at the sliding bolts at the top and bottom of the door, and the neon pink baseball bat just inside the door. Cooper had acquired the bat when he started getting involved with what some of my sister's friends in England might call *a different class of people*. When Cooper left, the bat remained, proving useful for Curtis over the next few weeks when a few of Cooper's so-called friends had appeared.

I debated whether to leave the sliding bolts open, but in the end decided to lock them. Curtis could wake me when he got home.

I carried on to the bathroom, entering without turning on the light so I didn't have to look at myself in the mirror. I grabbed the Tylenol from the medicine cabinet and retreated to the kitchen, where I started on my hangover-avoidance cure: two Tylenol and many, many glasses of water.

On the second glass I lifted my phone, still on its lanyard around my neck, and called Curtis. The ringing began in his room. I cursed under my breath: "That's why we called from my phone."

It was time for bed. I made a deal with myself: I wouldn't shower tonight, but instead I'd get up half an hour early tomorrow. I set the alarm on my phone and headed for bed.

seven

"At times like this I hate you, Curtis," I heard myself mutter.

The tapping at the front door continued. Not just a tap, but a rhythm. And then it paused.

I pulled the duvet tighter, hoping the noise was just my imagination and that it wasn't Curtis finally returning.

But the tapping started again. Again, the soft, gentle rhythm at the door...at the front door that I had bolted, meaning it could only be opened from the inside.

While my room was never going to be featured in *100 Most Desirable Homes* magazine, it did have one huge advantage when it came to sleeping: no windows. No windows meant no noise and no light coming in from the street. But that didn't stop the sound of tapping on the door, especially as the sound would then echo around the tiles and hard surfaces in the hall.

I surrendered and crawled forward on my bed, reaching out of the room and feeling for the light switch in the hall, which would perform two functions. First, it would let Curtis know that I was awake—with that knowledge, he could be patient. Second, it would shine some light into my room.

There was a light in my room, but it was a strip light. While the strip light performed its task admirably, it was ugly, and more importantly given how I was feeling, it was far too bright at the moment. I should have taken more Tylenol.

As the yellow light pushed its way in from the hall, I eased myself through the narrow gap between my bed and the washing machine and stood in front of the closet, looking for an oversized T-shirt—I wasn't in a mood for trying to protect my modesty with limbs and awkward poses, and exhibitionism wasn't my thing.

I closed my eyes to shield them from the light as I came out of my room, and as I walked I wrestled with the T-shirt. These things are meant to be simple to slip on, but apparently when you've just been woken and you're keeping your eyes shut, it's not that easy.

Arriving at the door, I half opened my eyes knowing that the light was behind me, and reached for the sliding bolts—first the one at the top of the door and then the one at the bottom—before I twisted the latch and gently pulled the door, half-closing my eyes as I turned back toward the light and my room.

"What time is it?" I asked, feeling my oversized tongue flopping in my mouth and not really expecting a serious answer from Curtis.

The door moved faster than I expected: the breeze created by its movement and the shudder of it slamming into the wall told me this. I felt a hand cover my mouth and an arm slide around my waist to hold me tightly, and a second person went past, heading toward the kitchen.

In the shock, my yelp was stifled by the hand over my mouth, but I was now awake. Very awake. With a thumping head and with my eyes now fully open, I felt the ache of my pupils in throbbing eyeballs reacting to the bright light.

The arm around my waist pulled me back toward the door. We stopped. I guess he balanced on one leg, using the other to flick the door, which shut behind me, and then he turned and maneuvered me against the wall. His arm was no longer around my waist, and the hand over my mouth, while large, was only placed there—no pressure was being applied.

"High five, sister. High five." His voice was rich but soft, his accent African, although I couldn't be more specific about his origin other than naming the continent.

I focused on the figure. He was tall, well built, and black, wearing jeans and a faded brown T-shirt. He placed his finger across his lips, then raised his eyebrows, questioning.

I frowned.

He slightly tensed the muscle in his hand over my mouth and lifted his eyebrows again. I nodded, and he let his hand fall away. Without his red robe, he was just a normal guy with a broad white ivory smile. "High five, sister."

A normal guy who had woken me and pushed his way, uninvited, into my apartment. I became aware that my breathing was fast, shallow...irregular, and that my heart was beating out a warning to anyone who would listen.

The other guy came out of the kitchen. He looked up at me—bloodshot yellow orbs. The black visage cracked to reveal two rows of yellow teeth—blackened around the gums, with several teeth missing—between two cracked and bleeding lips. He turned into the front room.

"Where's your boyfriend?" I turned back to the guy standing in front of me.

"Who?"

He tilted his head and sighed like a disappointed parent. "Where's your boyfriend?"

"I don't know." He was the disappointed parent—I was the surly teenager. "He went off. And he's not my boyfr..."

"Where did he go, sister? Where did your boyfriend go?" His tone remained calm, understanding. "We not going to hurt you—we just need your boyfriend."

"I don't know. There was a cop car outside. He panicked and left." The mention of a police car elicited the first reaction—a subtle widening of the eyes. Normally I would have missed it, but under the glare of the light and with his face being so close to mine, I noticed the increasing size of the two bright circles in his dark skin.

"I don't think I believe you." His voice was slower but still calm. He looked to the other man as he came out of the front room and said something—a few words in a language I didn't understand. The man who had been wearing the green-and-orange-checkered robe but who was now searching my apartment headed for Cutis's room.

The man who had been wearing a red robe made a clicking sound—a single click, he had my attention—and then continued: "Your boyfriend hurt our kin. He's in a coma at the hospital. You need to understand how serious we are about finding your boyfriend."

I shrugged and stood away from the wall, looking to see where the other man had gone and what he was doing.

"Where is your boyfriend, sister?" He moved to stand with his back to the door, drawing my eyes away from my search for the other guy.

Somewhere behind me a closet was opened and shut— red robe looked vaguely in the direction of the sound.

I didn't want my room invaded. I love my room. It's tiny, but I love it. When Cooper moved out, Curtis offered me the vacant room—he even said I could keep the same rent arrangement until we found someone permanent. But I didn't need the bigger room—mine is already big enough to hold everything I own, and although it was an ugly puppy, it was my ugly puppy.

And my ugly puppy wasn't going to be investigated. I didn't want a stranger poking through my things, so while red robe wasn't focused on me, I moved. Quickly. And ran for my room, shutting the door behind me.

There was a foot wedged between the door and the jamb, stopping it from shutting. I let out a yelp and scrambled onto my bed, pushing myself into the top corner of the room, pulling the duvet tightly around me.

Red robe let the door swing open and stepped in calmly. "Shhh. Relax, sister. We're not going to hurt you, but we need to talk with your boyfriend."

I looked to the guy, who had been cheekily bumping my ass a few hours ago. "Please. I don't know where Curtis is." The room was quiet apart from the sounds coming from the bathroom, where the search for Curtis had reached.

The doorway darkened. A voice came from outside the room. The man inside chuckled, and looked to me as he spoke. "No. He's not in here, is he?" Then he looked back to the man outside the room and clicked twice.

"You understand we're not after you," he said. "But I want

to see your boyfriend within twenty-four hours."

He turned and left. I heard the front door slam as I sat wedged in the corner of my bed, pulling my duvet tighter.

eight

"They want Curtis. They want Curtis," I quietly said to myself as I sat in the corner, pulling the duvet tighter around me.

"They want Curtis. They want Curtis." It was my mantra. I tried to repeat it in the hope that I would distract myself and fall asleep again.

I guess I sat in the half-light spilling from the hallway for fifteen minutes, but maybe it was half an hour—I hadn't looked at the time. My phone is my clock, and that was hanging on the back of my door when the unwanted visitors arrived.

When I did finally move, I went to the front door and locked the bolts. If Curtis was going to come in, then he was going to have to disturb me. Then I grabbed the neon pink baseball bat, took it back to my room, and dug out a clean pair of jeans, which I slipped on before I returned to check the front door, making sure I had slid the bolts all the way into place.

Carrying the baseball bat, I then proceeded from room to room, making sure the windows were firmly closed. I hadn't been particularly worried before I went to bed, but somehow I felt I wanted to check now.

The kitchen window was tight shut. In the front room I checked the two windows and the door that opened onto the balcony, then I pushed my face up against the glass, trying to look up and down the street. I half expected to see my visitors, black figures in a poorly lit street in the middle of the night, but there was nothing apart from a scooter zipping along the road.

The small window in Cooper's vacant room was secure, but the window in Curtis's room gave me pause for thought. It wasn't so much the pane of glass (which was solid) or the frame (which was secure), but the flat roof outside the window, which was an ideal platform for anyone looking to get in. Unlike the balcony at the front, there was no street lighting and no passing traffic.

I stared through the window, looking for any sign of humanity—friend or foe—but saw none.

I dragged the bat as I went to the bathroom. There was no need for the light there: I didn't want to have to look myself in the eyes—I'd just start asking questions—and I didn't need a light to pee and to wash my face.

Feeling the breeze on my slightly damp face, I returned to bed, taking the baseball bat and not removing my jeans as I got in.

After lying sleepless for thirty minutes, I went to check the doors and windows again, taking the neon pink baseball bat with me. I got up, but as I flicked the light on in the hall, I started to repeat my mantra: "They want Curtis. They want Curtis."

I didn't need to check the windows—I knew they were closed, and looking at them again wouldn't help. Instead I went back into my room and grabbed my phone. It was 3:29 AM. I called Curtis. The phone sounded in his room. I swore and hung up, then remained still, thinking.

I became aware of my feet feeling cold on the tiles. I looked at my phone: It was 3:34, and I hadn't worked out how to contact Curtis.

I stepped back into my room, returned my phone to its hook behind the door, then repeated my mantra, "They want Curtis." I replaced the baseball bat in its customary home by the front door and returned to bed, slipping off my jeans before I got back in.

I slept fitfully, gradually becoming aware that I was awake and there was no further sleep to be had tonight. I crawled out of bed and flicked on the light outside my room before throwing on a few clothes and grabbing my phone.

It was just past 4:30 AM.

I flicked through my call history, looking for the number

called shortly after midnight. As the phone started ringing, I began to walk. I was closing the front door as the voicemail picked up. "Hi, Youssef. It's Monty here. I'm trying to get hold of Curtis. Can you give me a call—on this number? Thanks."

By the time I had hung up, I was walking on the sidewalk. Within a minute my phone rang.

"Monty!" It was Youssef.

"Youssef, I need to speak with Curtis."

"You sound...worried."

"I just need..."

"Where are you, Monty? Are you outside? You sound like you're outside."

"I'm outside."

"I'm coming," said Youssef. "Where are you?"

"I'm...I'm walking toward that bar near the apartment where Curtis and I met you at once."

"I'll be there in three." He hung up.

He was actually there in four—I saw his black and yellow Toyota arrive as I was walking up. He was out of the cab and looking for me, the look of concern on his face receding as he realized the footsteps he could hear were mine. "Hey Monty," he said softly as he opened the passenger door for me.

He sat behind the wheel, hit the central locking, and switched on the light. I felt my eyes throb with a bright light for the second time that night. "What's up?"

"I need to speak to Curtis." Was I overreacting?

"I don't know where he is," said Youssef, "but I can tell you where I dropped him." I looked up, feeling a flicker of hope. "By the docks. The old part—near the fishing boats."

"Can you take me there?" I asked. "A black American guy with a limp is gonna stick out among the fishermen."

nine

Few people in Barcelona know where the fishing docks are. I only knew because Curtis had once asked me to pick up a package from there. The map he drew was detailed, directing me across the water from the back of Maremagnum—a manmade cluster of shops and nightlife designed to ensure one part of Barcelona never slept—and through the grimy docks covered in fish scales and netting. It seemed centuries away from the two marinas with the fancy yachts for the wannabe playboys to pose on, and the ferry terminals taking people to and from the Balearic Islands and providing a short-term stop for the Mediterranean cruises that passed.

Youssef insisted that I take his business card and show him that I had programmed his number into my phone—it wasn't enough that I had called him. Then he gave me €10 to buy breakfast.

By the fishing docks it was calm—not quiet, but calm. There was still a thumping from the nightclubs and bars, which periodically spewed drunk tourists who were then mopped up by the taxis waiting for them. When I left him, Youssef thought that was the best place to get his next fare.

I spent some time walking around the jetties between the old fishing boats. I didn't see Curtis. Instead I found the end of a jetty and sat, staring into the water, trying to make sense of the past few hours.

With the first light, but before sunrise, the heavy feet of the arriving fishermen—short, stocky men with silver hair and dark, parched skin—roused me from my contemplation. They were probably used to seeing drunk partygoers sitting at the end of the jetty and seemed happy to leave me. As I walked back, one said "good morning" in accented English. I smiled at the correct assumption and completed another circuit of the small fishing port, but didn't find Curtis.

After a cursory circuit of the yacht clubs, I gave up and went to find something to eat in a nearby café before I caught a bus heading northward, which would take me closer to home. I arrived at my stop just after seven. Getting closer to the apartment, I became aware of a nervousness... an apprehension.

As I reached our street, I found I was stepping so that my footsteps wouldn't make a sound. And I was slowing, with my head going back and forth like a windshield wiper. At the main entrance to our block, I decided to make another circuit of the block. I wasn't sure why—it was probably something else I'd seen in the movies.

I didn't see anything out of the ordinary. I didn't hear anything out of the ordinary. But there were more people around—the street was waking up, and if I screamed, I'm sure someone somewhere would've heard me.

I moved quickly through the entrance, past Ana's door and up the stairs, and waited—catching my breath and listening—outside the front door, the key in my hand. The lock was old—if you were gentle, it wouldn't make the zipping sound when you pushed in the key.

I opened the door an inch, took out my key, and listened. It was almost as if I could hear rustling. Almost, but not quite. When I first moved in, the door squeaked when it opened. This annoyed me enough that one night I put some olive oil on the hinge, and now the door glided open. I stepped in, cautious to avoid slapping my feet on the tiles, and pushed the door behind me without closing it, since the lock would click, alerting whoever was in Curtis's room to my presence.

They want Curtis. They want Curtis, I rationalized, internally repeating my mantra.

I remember when I was living outside Buenos Aires. I got home one day, and the family I was staying with were all standing outside—a rat had got into the kitchen. I'm no fan of rats, but a basic principle seemed appropriate to me: Human beings should be inside the houses that they own;

rats should be outside.

To me, there was a simple solution—open the door, then chase the rat out. As long as I didn't stand in the rat's way, I would be fine. When given the choice between me and the open door, the rat chose the door.

There was someone in Curtis's room. I could hear clearly: There was the rustling of paper, there was fabric moving against fabric, drawers were opening, drawers were closing, the floorboards and joists were grumbling as the weight they supported moved.

I reached to my left and picked up the neon pink baseball bat. I gripped the handle with both hands, feeling the weight, getting a feel for how it would swing—this was my home, and it was time to chase the rat.

The light in Curtis's room was shifting, but I couldn't tell if there was one person in there or two. And I couldn't tell whether there was anyone else in the apartment—there weren't any other sounds.

I took a step forward, paused, and surveyed.

Then another.

A third and I was by Curtis's door but unable to see into his room.

Deep breath. I stepped to fill the doorway, brandishing my club. "What the fuck, Curtis?"

There were two drawers on his bed and a large pile of clothes. On top of the chest of drawers where his phone usually rested—and still rested, but now had been joined by his door keys—there were stacks of ten-dollar bills, each stack weighted by a mug from the kitchen.

I repeated: "What. The. Fuck. Curtis?"

Since I had last seen Curtis, he had changed. Now he was smaller. Now he seemed scared. Now he was frozen and unable to reply. He stood holding a backpack.

Slowly he began to thaw, the side of his mouth twitching as if he thought a cheeky smirk could explain everything. A gust of wind fluttered the cash, bringing Curtis back to life. He stepped to the chest and began to place handfuls of cash into the backpack.

"Curtis!"

"What? It's money." There was little conviction in his statement. "It buys stuff."

"Was that what I carried when we went to the Sagrada Família last night?"

The bewilderment drained from his face, and he shook his head.

"Then what was I carrying?"

"Nothing serious, Monty. It wasn't drugs…"

"Wasn't drugs." I felt the tension in my throat, and I knew my hands were gripping the baseball bat hard enough to warp the wood. I tossed the bat onto his bed to reduce the chance that I'd beat him with it. "Why do you even bring up drugs? I thought we sorted that when Cooper went."

He continued placing small stacks of bills in his backpack. Another small gust blew through the window, and a few bills fluttered to the floor.

I bent to pick the bills and held them out for Curtis, looking as I passed the paper. "The fuck, Curtis!"

"What now?" he asked.

I pulled a bill back from his grip, showing him one side and then the other. The front, then the back. "I'm no expert on these things, Curtis, but conventionally greenbacks have a face on one side—usually a dead president—and something different on the back, not another dead president."

"Shit," Curtis spat under his breath, digging into his backpack. After a minute of rummaging he said, "It's only these three."

"Where did this come from?"

I looked directly at him. Curtis was busy flicking through his remaining stack of cash before he dumped it into his backpack and stuffed some clothes on top of the cash. "I don't have time to explain at the moment." He zipped up the backpack, then hitched it onto his shoulder before reaching for his phone.

"You don't come in here and…"

He held his finger up to his lips. "I don't have time." He paused, fixing his stare on me. "I'm getting out of Barcelona."

ten

"You're asking me to throw myself out?"

There was a trace of regret across Curtis's face. "You're right, Monty..."

"That I shouldn't make myself homeless?" I think my tone could best be described as terse.

"No... Yes... No... I mean..." Curtis paused, his eyes looking heavenward. "I hurt that guy—you said it yourself—and that's not the sort of hurt that gets forgotten in a day or so. I need to leave Barcelona...and if I'm not in Barcelona, then this apartment..." His voice trailed off. He shrugged and raised his hands in a "what are you going to do" motion.

I stood. Silent.

Curtis pulled out his phone, looked at the screen, and then returned it to his pocket. When he continued, his voice was soft, his demeanor apologetic. "Look, Monty, I know this puts you in a bind, and I'm sorry. Really, I'm sorry. But I can't pay for an apartment I'm not living in."

I knew he was right. I just didn't want have the hassle of finding somewhere new to live. The apartment was convenient, the room was cheap, and it would be a great place to stay for the next three or so months that I wanted to spend in Barcelona. But now, I'd have to find somewhere new. Short-term I'd probably have to book myself into a hotel or a hostel and put the word around that I was looking for a cheap room somewhere.

Hardly the end of the world, but it wasn't what I wanted.

"I'm not going to have time to go and see Juan, the agent," said Curtis. "You'd do me a real big favor if you'd go and get the deposit back."

My eyes narrowed: "You didn't use that double-headed money? I'm not going to get arrested, am I?"

"Nah. I paid in Euros." His voice brightened. "When

you're there, talk to him. Ask Juan if you can stay. He might let you have a week or so—tell him it's better to have someone in a place making sure no one breaks in..."

I stopped listening. I wanted to tell him that the guys were looking for him, but that would be reaffirm his intention to run.

Curtis scribbled on a piece of paper. "There's Juan's address." I pushed it into my pocket next to Youssef's card. "Make him an offer—make yourself useful, and he might let you stay. And if you want to keep the place and pay the rent, I'm sure he won't have a problem."

I still didn't like the change.

"I'll let you know when I know where I am, and you can hold onto the deposit until we can sort something out."

I felt a draft coming through the window—it interrupted my thoughts as I tried to explain to Curtis. What was I trying to explain? "But I... What if... How about... I don't want..."

Something changed across Curtis's face, and he lunged for the neon pink baseball bat that I had thrown on his bed.

An arm was being slipped around my throat. "High five, sister," a familiar voice purred in my ear, and the arm tightened, reaching a point where it was firm around my neck but was exerting no pressure.

I wriggled. I tried to punch behind me. I hit back with one shoulder, then the other. The grip remained unflinching. As long as I didn't struggle, there was no pain. When I struggled, the pain was self-inflicted.

"I'm sorry," he whispered in my ear, then began talking to Curtis. "You can't think this is unreasonable—you held my sister's boy far tighter and you made him piss his pants."

Curtis held the bat, tightening and loosening his grip, looking from me to the man who had worn the red robe yesterday evening and then back to me. Eventually, he spoke: "Let her go." He twirled the bat as if he were nervously waiting for the pitcher to release the ball.

"What do you want?" I asked.

"I want him, sister." His breath was warm on my ear. He raised his voice as he was talking to Curtis. "You put my friend in a coma." A pause. "My friend is in a coma in the hospital…because of you."

I didn't have a part in this conversation; it was time for me to leave. I threw my weight to the left. The bulk behind me counterbalanced as I threw my weight to the right before lifting my feet, taking all my weight on my chin, which I dug into the arm across my throat.

My weight pulled him forward, and I felt his grip tighten. As my eye line dropped, I saw Curtis swing the bat with some force, even though he was too far away to make contact.

There was a sound—like wood on flesh—and then I was dropped, with my captor falling on top of me, pinning me down. There was the noise of scrambling, and then a deep thump followed by a few steps and more scrambling.

My captor levered himself to a semi-upright position, grabbed the neon pink baseball bat, which was lying in front of us, and used it to help stand up. By the time I got to my feet—twisting the knots out of my neck and feeling my new bruises—red robe was turning away from the window.

"Where's Curtis?" I asked. He pointed through the window with the baseball bat.

"Did he take his bag?"

A single nod.

"Then he's gone, so you might as well leave."

I didn't see his response. My elbow ached—it had hit the floor, and then my captor had landed on it. I rolled back my sleeve to massage the joint. When I looked up, I expected him to be gone but he was rummaging through the top of Curtis's chest of drawers. He held up three ten-dollar bills, smiling broadly.

"Turn them over," I said.

He frowned.

"Turn them," I held out my hand, feeling my elbow twinge as I extended my arm. I turned my hand over: "Over."

He flipped the bills.

"Now look at them," I said, looking at my hand as I flipped it.

He followed, flipping the bills, and then threw his head back, laughing. "They are fake!"

He put the bills in his pocket and turned to stand directly in front of me, his eyes locked on mine. He dropped the bat on the bed, and a grin spread across his face as his eyes dropped to my chest. The hand that had been holding the bat reached forward and grabbed my phone. "In case he calls you," he said, lifting my phone and sliding the lanyard over my head.

eleven

I moved quickly.

I shut and locked Curtis's window, then went to my backpack under my bed and took out my three remaining phones. Three dumb phones that I had acquired from friends when they upgraded to smartphones. One of the three turned on, although its battery was pretty low. I took the phone, a spare lanyard, a charger, and my tattered address book and left the apartment.

No looking. No checking. I just walked as quickly as I could.

The first stop was a phone shop. I bought a new pay-as-you-go SIM card and loaded it with €20 credit. While I was in the phone shop, I toyed with the new smartphones—in truth, I was checking where the agent's office was located.

Having figured where I was going, I walked briskly to the office, which was on a side street with the entrance down an alley. The sign on the door said the office opened at 10 AM, so I found the nearest coffee shop, plugged in the phone's charger, and sat down.

The first number I programmed was my sister Ellen's—I knew the number without looking it up. I started hammering out a text: "lost my phone"—that wasn't untrue; I just didn't specify *how* I lost it—"this is my new number. Love Monty xx".

I hit send.

I took a sip of coffee and stared out the window, waiting.

The phone pinged—I checked the text message. "Again!!! :-) Hope Barcelona is still wonderful. Love Ellen xx".

I stared at the message. I wanted to go and see Ellen. To be with Ellen. But I also wanted to stay in Barcelona. Maybe after my lunchtime shift I would check out the price of flights. Perhaps I could spend a few days in London with Ellen.

I broke from my daydream and began to load my contacts. I started with Youssef, then went through my contacts book. Two phones ago, a guy saw me following this ritual. Once he stopped sneering at my "dumb phone," which was his opening gambit, he said I should look into cloud storage.

I *accidentally* spilled my coffee in his lap.

He still didn't seem to understand that, first, I didn't like him, and second, my system works perfectly well for me, as I was currently proving.

And yeah, it was childish to tip coffee over him, but it gave me a more interesting story.

Having plugged in my contacts, I checked the time. 9:50 AM. Ten minutes. I slowly finished my coffee and thanked the waitress as I placed my cup on the counter before walking back to the agent's office.

There was a white door with a central glass strip and security mesh behind. It wasn't properly closed, so I pushed it and stepped into the damp room, taking in the white walls and the cracked linoleum tiled floor, both hidden by the wooden filing cabinets and a pin board on the wall with property details hanging in plastic folders.

"Good morning." The man behind the only desk—an old dark wood desk, with the papers organized in strict rows and a typewriter to the side—stood, offering his hand. I tried to guess his age—probably in his forties, maybe past fifty—as I looked at his thick graying mustache.

"Juan?" He nodded. "I'm Montbretia Armstrong... I'm staying with Curtis Washington."

"Staying *with* Curtis?" It was a strange inflection, and Juan's mustache twitched as he spoke. I wasn't quite sure about the nuance of his question. Was he asking about Curtis's and my non-relationship, or was he trying to ascertain my residency status within the apartment?

"With, in the apartment, at, under the, I..." I shrugged.

It seemed like such a simple question, and still I couldn't answer.

"He didn't tell us. That's a breach of the rental agreement." He walked to the closest filing cabinet, his white short-sleeved shirt pulled tight as he reached into the top drawer, pulling out a file he dropped in front of him as he sat down again.

"I'm not really staying," I stammered, trying to recover the situation. "It's more that I stop by occasionally. I'm traveling, so I'm only going to be in Barcelona for a few months." He didn't look up from his file. "I've only really stayed for one or two nights...and I stayed when he wasn't there once...just to look after...keep an eye... It's not a problem...?"

Keeping his gaze focused on the file in front of him, Juan tilted his head to the right, twitching his mouth.

He stopped twitching and looked up. I tried to change the subject. "Curtis has been called away on business—I'm dealing with his things at this end." Juan looked suspicious. I blurted, "Can we terminate the rental and get the deposit back?"

"Miss...?"

"Armstrong. Montbretia Armstrong. Call me Monty."

"Monty. Right." He scribbled something in front of him. "I don't know you. I have no authority to accept instructions from you or to give you the deposit."

"But he's traveling," I said weakly, "on business."

Juan raised an eyebrow. "I can act on his written instruction," he offered, "but he will still need to give a month's notice and pay this month's rent, and depending on the condition of the apartment when it is released, there may be withholdings from the deposit."

He didn't seem to be trying to be unpleasant—it sounded like he was just trying to explain the situation, so I thought I'd try my luck. "So if I can't give notice, then Curtis has got the apartment until the end of the month. Is that right?"

He smirked—he had read me. "Yes. Curtis has got the apartment until the end of the month—but I would still like the rent that is due."

They want Curtis. They want Curtis, I thought and tentatively asked a question. "And if I wanted to rent the apartment—say for three months—how much would that cost?"

"Per calendar month," said Juan.

I bobbed my head. A single nod—I could feel the apprehension of even committing to asking the question. He noticed and tried to give a reassuring smile as he flipped some pages. He winced, then turned the file and pushed it toward me, resting his fingers above a figure. The pained look on his face seemed to grow darker as he indicated the number.

I did a quick calculation.

Pretty much all my bar earnings would have to go to cover the rent. If I wanted to eat, I'd have to dig into my savings. To buy new clothes—a new T-shirt for work—would cut into my savings. If I decided to get a bus to work or was lazy and got a cab home—savings. Insurance—savings. Local taxes—savings. If I took a day or two off and didn't get paid—savings.

No savings meant less traveling. The whole point of working, the whole point of living frugally, the reason I took the room and did the boys' washing, was to save money. In three months, I could spend a lot of money very quickly. In three months I could be less well off than I am today.

"I'd need a reference, too," he said. "One for you, and a financial reference to confirm that you are in permanent employment and can afford the rent."

"Can I think about it over the weekend?" I asked, even though I knew it was too expensive.

I stood and shook his hand, then left for work.

twelve

I worked the lunchtime shift at the tapas bar, and as I worked, my phone finished charging.

The shift was gloriously uneventful—just the regular crowd of people, eating and chatting. No one grabbed me. No one threatened me. No one questioned me about where Curtis was.

Most days I work two shifts: lunch and the evening. Between the shifts I like to get home, maybe have a shower, perhaps read a bit or watch the TV. Sometimes I send emails, and other times I write up a blog post so that I can tell everyone what I've been up to.

Whatever I do, it's my time, and I can always be sure that I've got the apartment to myself. Curtis is always out, and when he was staying with us, Cooper was usually out too.

Working two shifts makes a long day, but with the break in the middle, I've never found it that tough. And, of course, working two shifts means I can earn more money.

But as I shut the front door of the apartment behind me, something felt wrong. The apartment smelled different. It wasn't a bad smell—just different. And it was noisier—like the door onto the balcony at the front was open.

I slipped off my sneakers and turned into my room.

There was a noise. "Curtis," I said, turning back and walking into the front room.

"High five, sister."

The brown leather sofa ran across the window with a gap to get behind it and out onto the balcony. The door onto the balcony—the door I had checked before I left—was open. On the coffee table running in front of the sofa was a bouquet of red flowers—probably roses, but I wasn't going to look—wrapped in white paper.

"Get out!"

"No, sister." His voice was deep but light. The shake of his head slow.

"And how did you get in?"

"Curtis left his keys when he went out the window—I borrowed them." He picked up some keys on the table next to the flowers and held them between his fingers, as if offering proof.

"Sister. We have been fighting when we should be friends." He stood and held the flowers toward me. "My name is William. I am pleased to meet you."

"Where's Curtis?" I asked, ignoring the flowers.

William shrugged and gently waved the flowers as if I might have missed them. My phone—now my old phone—hung around his neck. William saw me looking at the phone. "He called. I answered. He hung up. I called back and he hung up, and now his phone has gone dead."

William returned the flowers to table next to the door keys and looked back at me. "You should put them in water."

I ignored him.

"Have you spoken to him?" His tone had lost some of the depth and had none of its earlier playfulness.

I shook my head.

"I believe when you tell me he is not your boyfriend, but you know he's going to contact you?"

"How can he?" I asked. "You've got my phone."

William took a step forward and cupped his finger under my chin, lifting my head until I met his gaze. He waited, staring at me, his breathing uneasy. "I need to talk to him, and I will talk to him, but that doesn't mean that you and I can't be friends."

"You take my phone. You've got my keys and you let yourself in, and then you want to be friends." I was surprised by my defiance.

He seemed to be weighing up how to respond, then shrugged, took the phone from around his neck, and placed it next to the flowers and the keys on the table. He stepped back, placed a hand on his heart, and bowed his head.

"Thank you," I mouthed, standing out of his path to the door. Then I thought again. "Take the phone." I picked it up and gave it to him. "That way you don't need to come back here."

thirteen

I pushed the door behind the man who called himself William and slumped down with my back to the door, gasping for breath, feeling my throat constrict and burn as I tried to inhale. It wasn't that I felt fear, more that it had been an emotional exertion to hold it together.

I liked the apartment—even if my room was tiny. I liked having Curtis around, even if he could be mysterious at times and a pain in the ass at others. I liked that I knew people in the block, even if that meant I had to deal with Ana's search for Mister Right more often than I wanted.

But William's visit was making me wonder whether I wanted to stay here. Even if I could swing a free stay until the end of the month because Curtis wasn't around to give notice, could I be sure that I would receive no further visits? Even though I had Curtis's keys, could I be sure that William hadn't taken a copy?

I wondered how long I would need to wait to be sure—if William didn't show up for the next week, was I in the clear?

When my ass went to sleep on the tiled floor, I figured it was time to get up and have a glass of water. As I finished the second glass, I decided I needed to talk to—or at least communicate with—Curtis.

A phone call was unlikely at the moment—Curtis didn't know my new number, and from what William said, his phone was now dead. But I could email him.

He kept his laptop under the bottom drawer in his chest of drawers. It wasn't much of a security precaution, but Curtis wanted it that way. Before seeing him with fake ten-dollar bills, I had been content to go along with his wishes—it was his computer, and I figured there's more to its value than the dollar amount it cost him, even if those dollars were double-sided.

But now I was hesitant.

Curtis had always been cool about me using his laptop. He knew I only wanted to do quick and easy stuff: check my email once or twice a week, post on my blog, maybe upload some photos, and do a bit of digging on the internet—checking maps, finding new places to go, booking flights, and confirming travel arrangements. Simple stuff. I'd turn on the computer, open the internet browser, and go. When I was finished, the browser would close, and I'd switch the machine off.

Before he first let me use the laptop, he said there was "y'know...stuff" on it.

He didn't elaborate, but we quickly found a solution by installing a second internet browser. I would use one, he would use the other, and that one browser would be all I used on the computer.

"That way you don't know what I'm thinking about buying you for Christmas," he said. In January.

I was happy with the arrangement. I made an assumption about the "stuff," and while it wasn't my thing, I was cool with whatever he wanted to look at as long as I didn't have to see it. And if Curtis looking at porn was the price for him not drilling holes in my wall and peering at me, then that worked for me.

The laptop ground to life. I opened my browser and clicked into my mail. It had been three, maybe four days since I'd last looked at my email, and there were 231 unread messages, including industrial quantities of spam. As I scanned the list, the third email hit me—it was from Curtis, sent four hours ago.

> HI MONTY. SORRY TO DROP THIS ON YOU. YOU ARE RIGHT I WENT TOO FAR AND THAT BIG DUDE TODAY CONVINCED ME. I CAN'T COME BACK TO BARCELONA SO I'M LEAVING. GOING TO TURKEY—WHY DON'T YOU COME TOO???

And then he made one of the smiley faces, as if that made it alright. "Like fuck am I going to Turkey," I muttered under my breath, although I had always wanted to go to Istanbul.

> SERIOUSLY! COME! IF YOU BRING MY STUFF, I'LL PAY FOR YOUR TRAVEL.

With fake bills, I thought.

> AND…

There were three smileys—not a good sign.

> I FORGOT MY PASSPORT. IT'S IN MY SOCK DRAWER. OOPS!

Oops! Oops? And yet somehow he seemed to have a plan to cross borders and leave Europe without a passport.

> I'LL EMAIL MY NEW ADDRESS WHEN I ARRIVE. TAKE CARE.

I was about to hit reply and send him my new phone number, but then it struck me: why? My heart said, "Just leave the stuff—Curtis can fix his own problem; you'll never see him again." But my head said, "It's a quick job to pack, and if you get the apartment clean, then you won't annoy Juan, and one day you might need Juan's help."

The voice that said I might need Juan's help won.

I was familiar with Curtis's clothes—I'd washed them all—and I'd seen his boots and sneakers. I knew he had a number of jackets: one leather and one olive military fatigue. I was sure he had more stuff, but I figured it would take me ten minutes to pack his gear, then I could shower and watch some TV. Plus with the drawers that Curtis had pulled out that morning, he had already started to help with the packing.

The sock drawer was one of the drawers that Curtis hadn't yanked out, so I decided to follow his lead and pulled it out before emptying the contents onto his bed.

I expected the socks.

I expected a passport.

I didn't expect three passports. I didn't expect what looked like a small stack of driver's licenses. And I didn't expect what looked like white powder in sachets. Without thinking I gathered up the sachets, passing the kitchen to grab some scissors before I headed into the bathroom.

I cut each sachet in half and dropped it into the toilet. Once they were all in the bowl, I flushed, then flushed again before the cistern had fully refilled, and squirted a liberal dose of bleach around the rim before shutting the lid and sitting down. "Think, Montbretia. Think," I muttered. Were those drugs? Were those Curtis's drugs? Was he dealing... supplying...whatever you do with drugs?

I looked at the blades of the scissors and couldn't see any powder, but I decided to wash them in any case, rubbing some antibacterial handwash over the blades before rinsing them down. I left the scissors on the sink and returned to Curtis's room.

Curtis's former room.

The first passport was an Italian passport in the name of Alan Albert White. The photo was of a Caucasian man I didn't recognize.

The second was again an Italian passport. This time I recognized the picture: It was my fellow American citizen, Curtis. Or Tennessee Albert Brown, as he was apparently called, which seemed an odd name for someone apparently born in Rome. I always thought Tennessee—as in Tennessee Williams, the only person I could recall with that name—was a sobriquet.

But then, I'm named after a flower and everyone calls me Monty. I suppose I shouldn't judge.

The third passport was from the States and again had a picture of the man I had called Curtis. James Marshall Williams, born in Tennessee, not Detroit, as Curtis had been. As Curtis said he had been...

I flicked through the laminated cards. All were European driver's licenses. One was in the name of James Marshall Williams and showed a familiar face. The other

faces—predominantly male, but some female; predominantly white, but some black, some Asian, some I couldn't
tell from the tiny photo—were unrecognizable to me.

As I flicked through the cards, I became aware that inside
an envelope one of these would feel very much like the
package Curtis had asked me to carry eighteen hours earlier.
"What are you into, Curtis?" I muttered. "If that is your real
name...and what have you gotten me into?"

Was this the rubbish I was meant to throw out? Or did
Curtis really expect me to carry this to Turkey?

There were three large holdalls—nylon tubes with
handles—beside the drawerless chest of drawers. I opened
them on the bed and started loading the clothes as I
pondered.

fourteen

I had been in Tierra del Fuego and, having missed Thanksgiving, I decided to spend Christmas and the New Year in London with my sister, Ellen.

South America had been great, but it was time to move on, and this time I decided on Europe. I could go to London at any time—there was always free accommodation and company with Ellen. Paris held little interest—I'd been there once, briefly. It was cold, it rained, and the wind cut through me. Germany and the Netherlands didn't seem a whole lot of fun in winter. I thought about Italy and I thought about Spain—it was time for me to stay in a big city by the Mediterranean.

I knew little about Barcelona; however, statistics that didn't mean much to me but that other people seemed to think were important kept cropping up: economically the fourth most powerful city in the European Union and thirty-fifth in the world, Europe's fourth best business city and fastest improving European city, and the fourteenth most *livable city* in the world, according to a lifestyle magazine. All that, and the port city had been established more than two-thousand years ago. Economics, livability, history. I decided to go.

I landed in Barcelona in the second week of January, spent the first night in a hotel and then got a place in a backpackers' hostel. Usually in a new place, I spend the first month doing the tourist thing and then find a job so that I can earn money and save up to do the tourist thing in the next place I visit.

On my sixth day in the city, I went on a tour. This tour appealed to me for three reasons. First, it was a walking tour. I much prefer the slower pace of walking: You can stop and look, unlike a bus tour that keeps moving unless it's in a traffic jam. Second, the tour was free: We tipped our guide at the end, which meant I could manage my costs. Third, the tour guide was a local—in this case, Valeria had lived in the city her whole life. And if there was a fourth reason: I'd already seen the Sagrada Família twice and wanted to see some other parts of the city.

On a chilly Thursday afternoon in January, my tour group comprised three of us: a couple from Copenhagen on their honeymoon and me. The couple...well, they should have gone back to their hotel. This meant that I had the full attention of Valeria. As we walked, we chatted, and she told me about her brother, Sergio, who ran a tapas bar. The previous night, his waitress—his ex-girlfriend—had quit. This left him needing a new waitress, but there was always the chance that the ex would want her job back, and trying to hire somebody who might be fired at any moment would be difficult.

I was happy to have a few days' bar work in Barcelona and could start that evening. Valeria called Sergio, and I got the job. Eight weeks later and the ex hadn't come back. I might not have a permanent contract—theoretically, I could be fired without notice—but Sergio has treated me well, and most importantly, he has always paid me.

From the moment I first walked into the bar and met Sergio, I loved it. I loved the calm. I loved the vibe. I loved how it looked, like my vision of an unpretentious tapas bar: not too big, dark wooden floor, wood paneling halfway up the wall with painted plaster above, and square tables with round-backed wooden chairs. I loved the people I worked with—I was treated as family. I loved the customers—they were quiet, respectful. Mostly men, although families do come in during the early evening. They were mostly older guys who worked blue-collar jobs and lived locally. They all came for the good food, a beer or two, and to have a chat. A bunch of unpretentious blue collars keeps the tourists away, which suited me.

From my first evening, the customers were so friendly,

so welcoming, and so forgiving of my awful Spanish. They were good at correcting me when I asked for help, even if most of what I was learning were words that could be found in any food store: chorizo, tortilla, and patatas bravas. But I also learned something of the wines and found that a shot of orujo was something I should avoid. And of course, taking money meant I got really good at counting in Spanish.

I'd put all of Curtis's clothes with his laptop, some papers, a few trinkets, and the fake IDs into three holdalls, which now sat in the front room. I'm not sure why I moved his bags there—somehow it felt better to clear his room completely. It then seemed like a relief to start my shift at 6 PM.

In my cocoon at work, I was able to reflect on Curtis's email. What did he mean: "oops"? Did he really want his passport—the passports—or was he saying I should destroy it? Or them? And what about the driver's licenses? More significantly, where was I going to live for the next three months?

The door opened, its characteristic squeal telling me that we had new customers to be attended to. I saw the bunch of lilies first: white lilies with their dark orange stamen, the dark orange pollen that somehow always manages to find its way onto white clothing—like my white T-shirt—and then stains it.

I looked up from the white flowers to see the dark skin with the ivory smile, and froze.

There was obvious discomfort among the regulars. They knew this guy wasn't one of their own. Like a cat when another cat crosses its territory, they were weighing up whether this new addition was a threat—and if a threat, whether it was better to fight or to creep into a corner and hide.

What I knew, but the customers didn't know, was that at this time of day, William would usually be getting ready to go out to work—or go out pickpocketing, as I saw it. That he was wearing the same jeans and T-shirt and not his red robe told me that because of a sequence of events which started last night when I tried to wind up Curtis, William's earning power had been greatly diminished. This loss of earnings was a pain many of the customers in the bar could understand, even if their stares suggested that they didn't realize what they shared in common with the newcomer.

With purpose, William walked up to me as I stood by the bar, still unable to move but realizing that the faces in the bar would be shifting their gaze from William to me. Me, the person to whom William was offering the lilies. Me, the person who could feel her cheeks starting to burn, and since my hair was pulled back in a ponytail, I couldn't hide my face.

He laid the lilies on the bar and stood in front of me, for the second time that day putting his finger under my chin to lift my eyes to meet his. "High five, sister. High five."

I could feel the customers looking away, trying to hide their embarrassment as William turned and walked to the door.

fifteen

The black and yellow Toyota was parked across the street from the tapas bar at 1 AM.

Normally I walk home. Normally I feel safe. Now? Now I was experiencing a tsunami of emotions—fear, guilt, anger, shame, indignity, incomprehension—that had crashed over and around me for the last few hours.

When I dropped the plate, I realized that I had been shaking since William's visit.

Sergio had seen William. He thought William was a misguided admirer. When the plate broke, Sergio sat me down and gave me a glass of wine. "I don't need anything to drink," I told him. "I don't want to get drunk."

"And I don't want you drunk." He pushed the glass toward me. "It's a nice wine. I want to know what you think." I believed him and sipped the wine as he went to clean up the mess I had created. It was only later that I realized he was being kind and making me sit down and think about something else.

Over the next three hours I calmed down. But by 12:30, I found myself trembling, so I called Youssef.

Youssef reached across and unlatched the door as he saw me coming. I got in and burst into tears. Like all good cab drivers, he was ready and pulled out a packet of tissues. Like all gentlemen, he shut up and let me get on with my blubbing, and then pretended nothing had happened and this was completely ordinary for him. He said one word: "Home?"

I nodded, feeling the next wave of tears.

I steadied myself, staring forward, fixing on the direction we were heading. "I had some unwanted attention today—it felt kinda..." Kinda what? How do you describe coming home and finding a man has let himself into your apartment?

"Then tonight, I thought I had rationalized everything… that I was calming down, but now I don't know if I feel safe."

It sounded so melodramatic. It sounded like—it felt like…it was—a gross over-reaction. I can look after myself, especially after several years of traveling, but I couldn't think what else to say. I didn't want to say anything more. Tonight had been embarrassing—everyone felt my embarrassment, and it was worse because I had people's pity, but I couldn't explain the intrusion I felt as my last bastion of safety was breached when William walked into the bar.

"Will you come and check that the apartment's safe?" I asked.

"Sure," said Youssef, holding his bottom lip between his teeth as his nodded. Three minutes later he pulled up around the corner from the apartment on one of the streets with enough space to pass parked cars.

He came around to my side and opened the cab door. When he shut the door behind me, I shrieked. It was only when I reacted like a gun had been fired that I realized how twitchy I was. I grabbed his arm, pulling him tight as we walked the short distance to the apartment block. At the front door I wasn't sure how to negotiate the entrance—we couldn't both fit, and I didn't want to go first in case someone was there. But I didn't want to go second and be left behind. Instead, we squeezed through together, somehow managing to pass without making any noise that could alert Ana.

I shut the front door behind us, sandwiching myself between Youssef and the door as I slid the two bolts, before I picked up the neon pink baseball bat.

I pushed Youssef into my room and followed him in even though there was barely space for both of us. The door was flat against the wall, but I still snuck a peak behind it. I pointed to the built-in closet that faced the doorway. I knew it had shelves and was shallow, but I still needed to be sure.

Youssef went for the handle and I raised the baseball bat. He turned to me, his jaw locked, his eyes wide. I threw my head forward to point at the closet and held the bat up to show him I was ready—he seemed to relax and exhale, his face softening before he turned to open the closet.

It was exactly as it had been the last time I shut the closet door: washing powder, cleaning sprays, toilet rolls, the towels and bedding the apartment had somehow accumulated, and my clothes. "Up there." I pointed to the top shelf—an unlikely hiding place, but I needed to be sure. Youssef looked to me as if asking permission. I nodded and he stepped on the second shelf, pulling himself up to look at the top shelf and then dropped down, shutting the closet doors.

"In the machines," I said, pointing to the washing machine and the dryer. Youssef shrugged and looked in both before standing upright and looking toward me. I was still holding the bat, ready to strike—it seemed as good a way as any to check my bed. A few not too hard, but hard enough blows were enough to convince me that no one was in the bed and no one had cut a hole in the mattress to hide.

"Under," I said. Dutifully, Youssef dropped to his knees, then lay on his side looking under the steel-framed bed.

He stood up, straightening his olive and tan pullover. "It's clear."

"You promise?" It sounded ridiculous, and I felt ridiculous asking, but I needed to be sure. I needed to know that I was being paranoid and everything really was fine. I needed to know I could lock the door after Youssef left and everything would be back to normal.

"It's clear," he repeated.

I dropped to my knees, reaching under my bed, and pulled out my small backpack, flattening it on the ground before I grabbed my big backpack, which was partially filled. I poked it a few times with the baseball bat, then reached for my boots and reached inside each in turn.

"Are we looking for a rat?" asked Youssef, seeming confused.

"Sort of," I said. "Come on." I backed out of my room, leaving the backpacks and boots scattered on the small square of floor in my room, and pushed Youssef into the bathroom.

He stopped still, his head scanning the room.

I held my hands together in front of me at chest height, gripping the baseball bat as I felt a drip of perspiration make its way down my back. "Anything?" I asked.

"Not that I can see," his voice echoed in the unpadded bathroom.

Next was Cooper's room.

Youssef knew the routine by now, and this room was easy. I had cleaned it after Cooper left, so there was nothing left apart from the bed and the wardrobe. Youssef opened the wardrobe with a flourish and looked inside, exaggerating his head movements to show he had looked in each corner. He went to the bed, patted it down, and then looked underneath.

"Nothing," he said.

"Could you check the window?"

He went to the single window, opened it, and then closed it again, giving it a shake to prove it was securely shut. He stood by the window, waiting. I nodded, and he led toward the next room, Curtis's.

Given that I had packed all of Curtis's belongings, I was happy to lean on the doorframe as Youssef checked the room.

He rattled the window. "All clear." I looked up—he was walking to the kitchen. "Every cabinet?" he asked.

"Every single one," I said absentmindedly, beginning to relax. It took him less than thirty seconds, after which he headed into the front room.

He saw the holdalls containing everything Curtis owned and a few other pieces that I didn't know what to do with. I could see him processing—he had seen my room and the other two bedrooms, both of which were stripped. "Is someone leaving?"

"Curtis."

"Is that why...?" He stopped himself.

I felt a smile—there were too many permutations that he could be constructing in his head. "No. That's not why I'm..." I paused, trying to figure out how to explain that Curtis and I might or might not be cool, but whatever the case, that wasn't what was upsetting me now. "Curtis had to go. This"—I pointed with no direction—"is different."

He half smiled, then set to work. He felt the holdalls; tipped the sofa and the chair over, peering underneath; looked behind the curtains and under the table; and checked the windows and door. "Nothing," he said with a nervous smile. "Where would you like me to check next?"

"That's... That's fine. That's all I needed. You've been more than kind."

"Do you want me to stay?" He seemed shocked by the forwardness of his own question. "I mean, I could sit in this room while you sleep."

"No, really. You need to get to work."

"But..."

I stepped into the hall. "I've got your number—you know I'll call."

A single nod confirmed his agreement. I placed a kiss on his cheek and whispered "thank you," sliding both bolts after the door shut.

sixteen

There was a tap on the door.

I had a look to see what Youssef had left—I figured he'd dropped his car keys or his credit cards when he'd been scrabbling on the floor and digging in the closets, and had realized as he got to his cab and come straight back. As I walked from room to room, I could hear the soles of my sneakers slapping on the floor—the high-pitched echo fluttering.

The tapping on the door continued.

This wasn't just tapping—this was rhythm.

This was a beat.

This was the beat I heard on a drum yesterday evening. This was the beat without the ornamentation, without a drum to give the nuance, without the interplay with the second drum...without the chanting.

I stared at the door, trying to catch my breath and willing that the person on the other side of the door hadn't heard the noise I had been making.

"Let me in, sister." The voice—with its heavy African accent—was low and gentle. Then the door groaned in the same way it groans when I lean on it as I'm leaving to make sure it's properly shut.

There was a low thump. The sound of flesh hitting wood... the sound of someone trying to force the door. "Sister. Let me in."

I hoped he couldn't hear my heart, which felt like it was making enough noise to wake the whole block.

"I know you're in there, sister—if you weren't, then the door wouldn't be bolted."

"Shit," I mouthed.

"Sister?"

"Go away." I was surprised at how calm my voice sounded.

"Sister, I'm not trying to make trouble, but my kin is lying in a hospital bed—he probably won't make it. If you call the police, then all they'll do is find the person who was there when my kin was beaten. If one of your neighbors calls the police...same result." The rhythmic tapping started again. "Sister?"

"I haven't seen Curtis," I said.

"Look me in the eye and tell me that, sister." I paused, calculating. If I walked away from the door, he'd break it down. If I did what he wanted, then he'd leave like he did last time I asked him to. "Look me in the eye and then I'll go, sister."

I could smell the alcohol as I cracked the door. My feet were firmly planted on the floor; my shoulder was behind the edge of the door, stopping him from pushing the small gap open. "Please. Curtis isn't here. I can't help you."

Every time I'd seen William, he had taken care of his appearance. When he was with the drummers, his red robe was like a peacock's tail. When he had been wearing jeans and a T-shirt, these had looked clean and ironed. His skin had always looked young, taut, and vibrant.

But now, his T-shirt was streaked with dirt and his face had lost its glow.

I thought he might be turning to go. I was wrong. He was turning to position his shoulder against the door. With one solid consistent push he was inside, closing the door behind him and softly panting.

"Where is he?" he asked.

"I don't know—you were there when I last saw him, and you've got my phone."

"I tried to be nice, sister. I bought you flowers." He sighed. "You must know where he went. Just tell me."

I shook my head, unable to think of anything to say.

"Then if he's not here, there's no one to protect you. And you're not going to the police because...well..." He let the suggestion of jail hang in the air. "So it seems like you've got to be nice to me. High five, sister. High five."

seventeen

It happened fast.

William had pushed his way in—he was after Curtis. Then there was the knife and he was looking around. Expecting, or maybe just hoping to find Curtis, ready with his knife.

And then I was pinned against the wall outside my bedroom, obliged not to scream because—he was right—I didn't want to the cops involved. With Curtis out of the country and about to be out of Europe, I was the only one who could explain the beating that led to William's kin, as he was now being called, being in a coma.

But there was the knife.

And he was taller than me.

And he was stronger than me.

And he had been drinking.

And he was angry.

And he was ready for violence.

I knew the neon pink baseball bat was close—I needed to get two steps and it would be in my hand. I played rock paper scissors in my head. The rock: my bat. The paper: his hand. The scissors: his knife. I couldn't win, and I had a lot to lose.

"I don't know where Curtis is—I can't help you." It was all I could offer.

"I don't believe you, sister." He pushed the knife against my throat as if he needed to reinforce the point.

"Please." My voice was hoarse. "You don't need to..."

He leaned his body against me, holding me against the wall, and eased off the pressure on the knife. I could feel his heart as his chest pushed my arm. Where I thought he would be calming, his heart seemed to be beating faster, and the sour blast of his drink-infused exhalation was becoming more rapid.

And there was an unwanted lump resting against my hip.

I moved my hip. He moved closer to pin me tighter. I moved my hip again. He moved closer again. The lump was getting bigger and moving. His cock knew where his body wanted to go—it was only a matter of time before his brain and his knife caught on with the idea.

He shifted his foot, releasing the pressure on me. I shifted. He thought I was running and pushed me into my room, following straight behind. There was a ripping sound—my blouse. I looked down to see his hand pulling the fabric and the knife returning to my throat.

He was panting. The smell of stale alcohol was being forced up my nostrils with each breath. I held my breath and willed my heart slower. Slower. Slower.

"It doesn't have to be like this," I said softly.

He noticed something had changed in what I was saying. "It can be different."

"You're just playing with me, sister." Something in his voice told me that he thought I was trying to humiliate him, but he wanted to believe otherwise.

I pushed my chest forward, bumping my boobs on him to move him back so he filled the doorway, and slipped my jacket off my shoulders before letting it drop to the floor. It still had Curtis's blood on it, although I felt it best not to bring that up. I kicked off my sneakers, then looked him straight in the eye and held his gaze as I reached to the waist-band of my jeans. His pupils were dilating—this was more than the alcohol.

He struggled to keep his gaze locked on mine and failed. I could hear his breathing becoming heavier.

"I'm serious." I rested my thumb inside the belt of my jeans, letting the weight of my arm tug at the waistband. "Very serious." His eyes fell from my chest and dropped to my thumb. "Very, very serious. But I'm not sure if you're serious."

"Uuuhhh..." he mumbled. "I'm seri..."

I pulled my thumb out of my waistband and snapped my fingers, breaking his trance. "Then we need to be clear." He stared at me, transfixed. "One night. One night that I promise you won't forget, and then you're gone. I don't know where Curtis is, so you can't keep coming here—but I can give you a going-away present."

I dropped my hands to the front of my waistband and undid the button.

His eyes followed.

I refastened the button and put my hands on my hips. His eyes lifted to meet mine. "One night, and that's it."

A single nod, and his eyes dropped to my jeans' button.

"Put the knife away."

The knife disappeared. I undid the button. "First, I need to pee." I stepped forward.

He stood firm.

"Come on. It's there." I pointed. "I can't get out of the bathroom—there are no windows."

I pushed him gently on the center of the chest. He stepped out of the room, far enough for me to squeeze through and get into the bathroom, where I closed the door, silently locking it behind me. The door wouldn't survive the first kick, but the lock would stop him walking in on me.

There were too many thoughts in my head. The simple answer was to run, but that was too much of a risk—he would catch me. And if he didn't catch me, then I would have lost everything. All my clothes, my money, my bank cards, details of my bank accounts. Would William look through my papers, find Ellen's number, and call her to say that I was missing...or wanted for a crime? Would William call the cops? What happened if his kin died? Would I be an accessory to murder? And now that I knew Curtis wasn't a pure as the driven snow, what else would be on his computer? What would the cops find if they looked at the computer and would they link it to me? I had probably used the computer for more time than Curtis. Would they believe it wasn't mine?

"Sister?" I jumped at the tap at the door.

eighteen

I cracked the bathroom door, pushed my head through the gap, and smiled weakly at William. "I know this sounds silly, but I'm a bit self-conscious about having someone... listen while I...you know..."

He stood immobile.

"Why don't you go into the bedroom and get ready—I'll only be a few moments."

He seemed ready to turn, but then his face became serious. "This is a game, sister."

"Then lock the front door," I said. "There's a sliding bolt at the top and the bottom."

I cursed silently as he called my bluff and turned to the door. I heard the bolts slide and smiled at him as he came back, turning into my room.

I shut and locked the door again and called Youssef. The call went straight to voicemail. I moved away from the door and whispered quickly. "Youssef. I'm in deep trouble. Shit like you would not believe—I need your help. Get here please. Please. Honk your horn when you arrive—three times so I know you're here—then wait outside." I was about to hang up, then I had another thought. "Don't ring this number. Thanks, Youssef. I owe you so much."

I felt my heart pounding and sat on the edge of the bath, taking gulps of air.

I stood and pushed my phone into my pocket. I reached for the door lock, then smiled at my mistake and turned, flushed, and rinsed some water over my hands. As I padded into my room, William came forward, seemingly struggling with the dilemma of where to touch me first. It took me a few seconds to realize that he was totally naked. My eyes glanced down—totally naked and getting increasingly excited. I reached out my hand and placed it firmly on his chest. "I'm in control."

He frowned.

"We can fight and it will be over quickly. Or we can do it my way, and I'll give you a night you won't forget."

He was still frowning.

"It's a simple decision." I tried to keep my voice soft and hoped he couldn't hear my pounding heart. "Do you want a night you'll never forget?"

I let the thought hang. His head nodded—more an enthusiastic tremble. He was probably guessing that he would get what he wanted faster if he just said yes.

"So we've got agreement?" His head was still doing the trembling thing. "I will give you a night you won't forget." He tried to push forward. My hand held firm. I turned my head so I could look at him sideways, giving my best schoolmistress look. "I'm in control. Do you understand?"

He nodded.

"And I'm in control—so we're doing things my way, and at my speed." My voice was slow, soft, gentle, like I was talking to a five-year-old child who knew a surprise was coming—and to whom I wanted to give a surprise—but who I was forcing to wait.

He nodded again, although I wasn't sure if he was really agreeing. "Take off your clothes, sister." It was an order, not an invitation.

"Slow down," I said, trying to keep the tension out of my voice while letting him see that my eyes were working their way down his chest. "We need to look after you first." I looked back up at him—there was a proud grin on his face. "And I need to get my rubbish out of here."

He frowned.

I forced a smile. "Come on, up on the bed." I patted the end of the bed. "Kneel here."

The frown turned to shock.

I patted the bed again. "I told you...a night you won't forget." I raised my eyebrows, hoping this would look more natural than the smile I still had forced across my face.

Cautiously he moved himself onto the bed and knelt facing toward me—the end of the steel bedframe separating us. All I could see in his face was nervousness and distrust.

Nervousness and distrust, mixed with anticipation.

I dropped to my knees. His eyes widened and his cock twitched as my head drew level. "All in time," I whispered to him and looked back to the floor where my jacket, backpacks, sneakers, and boots were scattered around the small area of my floor, with his clothes dumped on top.

Somewhere in this mess was his knife. He knew where—I didn't—but at a guess, it was in his jeans. I reached to my smaller backpack next to his jeans, and his hand grabbed my wrist. "What's up?" I asked, my voice registering shock.

"What are you doing?" he asked. His excitement was waning.

"I told you—I'm getting my rubbish out of here." I picked up the small backpack that I knew was empty and tossed it through the door before reaching for my boots and sneakers, and threw them, one after the other, to follow the backpack.

I looked at William, his hand securely but not tightly around my wrist, and hesitantly began to stand. With my free hand I moved my larger, half full backpack to rest on the door frame. "I'm going to open the closet now," I said.

"Why?" asked William, a lingering hint of suspicion in his voice, his grip looser.

"That would spoil the surprise," I said opening the closet door farthest from William with my free hand. I gently tugged the arm he was holding. He dropped his grip, allowing me to open the other door. I removed the cleaning materials—cleaning sprays, a feather duster, polishes, and polishing cloths—putting them on the dryer so that I could reach the sheets.

I pulled out a sheet and was about to open it when I looked back at the feather duster. It was a risk—and it was going to raise the stakes considerably—but if it worked, then it would put me back in control.

I picked up the duster. William looked as if he wasn't

certain whether he was confused or worried.

In my experience, a man with an erect penis wants one thing. Indeed, a man with an erect penis is generally thinking with the erect penis and no other part of his anatomy. And as long as William stayed erect—if only partially—I could stay in control, and he wouldn't ask any questions. The moment that boner disappeared, I was going to have problems.

I clicked, twice, to get his attention, in the same way I had heard him communicate with the other guy when they first visited the apartment. William looked up, his eyes widening. I held his gaze, then flicked his cock with the feather duster.

The broad rows of ivory told me I was on target. He laughed and then lunged forward as if trying to embrace me. I stepped back and pushed him away. "I'm in control, remember?" I said and stroked his cock twice with the duster. Gauging by his physical reaction, he was only going to be able to think about one thing. "See what happens when you leave me in control?"

He moaned softly.

I stroked him once more with the duster. He moaned again.

I put down the duster and shook open the sheet. In my softest voice asked, "Where's your knife?"

"Sister?" There was confusion in his question, but not aggression.

"If that's too difficult," I mumbled and stepped out the room. He kicked the dryer as he tried to get off the bed to scrabble on the floor. He said something. His voice was raised, but I wasn't listening—I was checking the bolts on the front door. Both the top and the bottom bolt had been pushed home. Obviously I could open them, but there was the question of time—unless I was lucky I wouldn't be able to slide both bolts, open the door, and get out before he reached me. And even though he might be naked, there was still a knife somewhere.

From the street a car horn blasted three times. I tried not to relax. I tried not to let my concentration slip. I tried not to show any sign that I was reacting to the horn.

I turned back to William. He was totally naked and standing just outside my room, holding his jeans. "Have you got the knife?" I asked. Sheepishly he withdrew it from his jeans. "Open it and hold it," I said. "Hold it tight."

Still somewhat confused, he complied.

As William held the knife toward me, I took the sheet, pulling it across the blade and tearing it into broad strips. William was still perplexed, but he seemed to enjoy the ripping and watching me move with speed.

When I had five strips, I stopped and took the knife from William, casually throwing it behind me. It hit my empty backpack as it landed with a clunk. "We don't need that anymore," I said to William, who had to divert his gaze from following the knife. "Give me your wrist."

He jumped as I took his wrist, lifting it to chest height. "Sister?"

"Shhh," I said, putting a finger across his lips. "Remember, you're going to get a night you won't forget."

He smiled goofily and offered no resistance as I tied the first strip around his wrist. I lifted his other wrist and mirrored the fabric attachment. "Now go and lie down," I pointed to my room with my eyes. As he lay down, I picked up the feather duster and gave him a few quick strokes. He responded with a spasm that told me he was very hopeful.

I gently flicked and tickled his cock again—William moaned and his erection stood firm while I contemplated my next move. It was hardly chess, but the stakes were rather higher for me. I put down the duster and moved between the washing machine and the bedframe, then lifted my foot before placing it on the other side of William's torso and slowly moved myself to sit on the bottom of his ribcage, but with my weight still held by my legs. Suddenly his arms were up, his hands were reaching out.

"Whoa, boy!" I pushed his arms down and leaned forward to tie to the bedframe the loose end of one strip of fabric that I had already attached to his wrist. Then I tied the other and looked down and smiled at William. For the first time that evening, it was a genuine smile. I smiled because his arms were tied to the bed. I guessed he thought I was smiling for another reason.

Cautiously I lifted myself off and admired my handiwork while absentmindedly stroking his cock with the feather duster again.

I reached through the bars at the bottom of the bedframe, grabbed his ankles firmly, and pulled. He slid downward, pulling his arms straight as his legs came through the bars at the bottom. It only took me moments to fix him in position with two more strips from the sheet.

Now he was secure.

I took the final strip and moved up between the washing machine and the bed, moving my head close to his, and whispered in his ear: "Now I'm going to give you the night to remember that I promised." He gave the goofiest grin I've ever seen. "I need to get ready first, and I can't have you seeing the magic." The look of confusion crossed his eyes, but he soon understood when I put the strip across his eyes and reached behind his head to tie it.

It only took one stroke of the feather duster to return the grin to his face.

I opened the closet and grabbed an armful of clothes. In the hallway I picked up my larger backpack and stuffed the clothes in. I managed two other armfuls of clothes between my two backpacks, throwing out anything that I could see would be easy to replace or was just excess bulk. In my final visit to the closet, I stood on the second shelf to reach the top shelf and recovered my passport and my supply of emergency cash. I dumped them both into my left boot and cautiously placed the knife in my right boot.

"I'm just going to have a quick shower," I said, William responded, but I didn't hear what he said as I shut the door.

I dragged my packs to the front room, grabbing my sneakers as I passed, and walked out onto the balcony. Some sweat pants had to be jettisoned to make room for the sneakers before I could fasten the pack closed.

Youssef had managed to pull his Toyota between the steel posts across the road so that traffic could still pass, and was resting on the hood of the car, looking up. He stood as he saw me get to the balcony.

I hefted the first of Curtis's holdalls onto the balcony, then dropped the bag over the rail, cringing at the dull thud as the stuffed nylon hit the ground. By the time I was dropping Curtis's third holdall, Youssef was standing under the balcony. I passed my two bags down and said softly: "Get the engine running."

I closed the balcony doors, picked up my boots and my jacket, and switched off the light.

nineteen

"Are the bags in the trunk?" I don't know why I asked. I don't know why I didn't say something graceful, like "thank you for saving me...again."

Youssef swung the door open as I padded over, feeling the stones through my socks. I put my boots into the front well, asked my stupid, thoughtless question, and slipped on my jacket before sitting and brushing down my feet.

"Are you okay?" asked Youssef.

"I am now that you're here," I said, trying to make sure he understood that I was grateful—not simply using words, but actually being grateful. "But can we get out of here quickly?"

We passed through a few back roads, moving swiftly, but I guessed staying close to the speed limit. We hit a main road, and he joined it. "Where are we going?"

"North."

I pulled out my phone: It was 1:30 in the morning, and I had no missed calls and no text messages. I slipped the lanyard around my neck and dug around in my boots, pulling out the cash and the knife. "Can you pull over at the next trashcan you see?" I asked, slipping on my boots but not tying the laces.

Thirty seconds later, Youssef hit the brakes and pointed. Set back from the road was what I wanted. I jumped out, wiped down the outside of the knife with my jacket, and dropped the weapon into the trash. As we pulled away, I passed Youssef €100. I tapped his thigh with the bills: "This is the first installment for tonight's ride."

He shook his head. "No, Montbretia. You know I won't take your money."

I laughed. It was the first time I had laughed properly in what felt like years but was probably only hours. "You don't know where we're going yet. So you're taking the money, and you're going to take more—but I'll have to make a bank transfer for the balance."

I left the cash on his lap, and he didn't argue.

We drove for about ten minutes in silence, and then I said, "Can we stop at the next gas station?"

"Sure."

"Fill it to the top," I said to Youssef as we pulled into the gas station. While he did that, I went to the shop and bought a five-liter plastic gas can. "Fill that, too." I went back into the shop and paid for the gas, a set of screwdrivers, and some matches. On the way out, I spent a few minutes looking at one of the road atlases.

"You didn't have to pay," said Youssef as I got back into the cab.

"I did, really, I did."

He started the cab, slowly moving off. "North?"

"How are you for a long drive?" I asked.

"Sure, where?"

"Perpignan."

"Perpignan?" It was a question.

"Perpignan, France." I said. "Two-hundred kilometers— about two hours there, two hours back. You should be home by six." Youssef accelerated. "I want to be outside the grasp of the Spanish police."

Youssef shrugged. "Okay."

"And when we get clear of the city, can we pull off the road when it's safe?"

He flashed a look at me. "Sure." He said "sure," although his tone said "why?" But still he kept driving.

We were half an hour out of the city as we drifted into a pullout beside the main highway. "Is this the sort of place you want?" It felt like we were on the top of a mountain with only an unlit strip of blacktop for company. I couldn't imagine a more perfect place.

"Can you flip the trunk?" I said, getting out of the car.

By the time he had decided to see what I was doing, I had Curtis's laptop, the three passports, and the driver's licenses, and had levered the hard drive out of the laptop—or at least what I thought was the hard drive. "Do you want a screwdriver set?" I asked, passing the screwdrivers that I no longer had a use for to Youssef.

"Thanks," he said. He didn't seem to want the screwdrivers, but I guess he was taking them to be kind.

"This is the hard drive, isn't it?" He shrugged. "Can we run it over?"

"You want to smash it?" he asked.

"Yeah."

"What about the tire iron? That would do a much better job!" I wasn't sure I'd ever seen him so animated. He disappeared into the trunk for a moment, pushing the luggage out the way, and then stood proudly with a tire iron in his hand. "Totally smashed?"

I nodded. He took the drive, dropped it on the ground, and pounded it with the tire iron before picking up the mangled wreck and offering it back to me. "Enough?"

I picked up the laptop without a hard drive and held it open—the screen and keyboard forming a V. "Drop it in there." I scanned the area—there was a semi at the far end, but apart from that it was deserted. "We need to make a fire," I said. "How about over there—away from the semi? Bring the gas."

I picked up the passports and the driver's licenses. In the end, my decision about Curtis's email dilemma was easy: If the documents weren't important enough for Curtis to take with him, then they weren't important enough for me to get arrested carrying them.

Youssef had the green plastic gas container with him when he caught up with me. "What are we doing?" he asked.

We reached the edge of the pullout away from the road. I placed the laptop V down and looked over the edge of the curb to find some small rocks to balance the computer. When it was secure, I put the passports and the licenses in the groove on top of the smashed hard drive. "We're getting rid of things that don't matter enough—and things that might cause a problem if anyone sees." Youssef looked slightly shocked. "Could you pour some gas on that?"

"That?" he asked. "The computer?"

"The computer that you smashed," I said. "Pour away."

Youssef poured some liquid over the small heap, and the smell of gas filled my nostrils. "Stand back," I said, lighting a match. It blew out immediately. I lit a second match, holding it at arm's length, and dropped it onto the pile, swiftly pulling my arm away and jumping back.

It caught immediately, and the smell of gasoline was rapidly replaced by the smell of burning plastic.

"Keep throwing on the gas," I said. "Keep throwing on the gas until it has all burned through."

twenty

I fell asleep within minutes of getting back into the car.

"Gare routière," said Youssef, gently waking me. The car wasn't moving.

"Huh?"

"Central bus station," he translated. "And that's the TGV station over there."

"Where are we?" My neck was hurting from my head hanging forward.

"Perpignan...France...the bus station." He paused. "Do you want me to take you somewhere else? Or I can wait with you..."

"What time is it?" I was still having trouble with being awake.

"Four AM," he said without drama and got out of the cab, closing the door quietly behind him. He was back in a few moments. "It's hours until any buses pass through, but there is a waiting room."

I sighed.

"Or you can stay here."

"No. Help me with the bags—you need to get home." I opened my door without looking and let my first foot fall to the ground. The fug of the car was replaced by the clean chill of the French air.

By the time I had stood up and got around to the trunk, Youssef had carried two of Curtis's holdalls to the waiting room. For the third visit to the waiting room, I carried my small backpack, and he lugged my large one and Curtis's last holdall.

As we got into the waiting room—an aluminum and glass box with concrete floors and steel benches bolted to the floor, empty apart from the two of us—I arranged the bags to form a bed. "I'm going to have to buy a second seat on the coach to carry this lot."

He smiled and then broke his usual vow of nonintrusion. "So what now?"

"I'm going to see Curtis. A lot of stuff has gone on...I've found out a lot of things...and I need to get everything straight. I deserve an explanation, and I want to have that conversation face to face."

Now that he'd asked the question, Youssef wasn't sure what to do with the answer. I filled the space to save his embarrassment. "And if Curtis has gone somewhere interesting, then I might hang around. How do I know if I'll enjoy a place until I've been there? Some destinations I've planned and I've loved. Some destinations I've planned and I've been disappointed. And sometimes I've just gone somewhere because that's where I ended up—it was a cheap flight, or I went to change buses and liked the city."

He seemed relieved not to have to think anymore.

"Have you got a pen?" From nowhere, he produced a stubby broken ballpoint. I pulled a piece of paper out of my pocket, checked the address on it, and then wrote down my email address. I showed him the piece of paper, pointing to the email address. "Send me your bank account details, and I'll transfer some more money over for tonight."

"No. You can't," he said.

"I'm not coming back—well, not this year, not next," I said. "I can't repay your kindness, but you must let me pay for you costs."

He stood speechless.

"And I've got another favor to ask." I took the apartment key out of my pocket and handed it to him with the scrap of paper. At the top was the address of the agent that Curtis had scribbled for me. "Take this key and go and see the agent tomorrow morning. His name's Juan and that's his address. He opens at 10 AM. Tell him there's an urgent rodent problem in the laundry room. He needs to get on it first thing tomorrow...I mean today."

"Okay," said Youssef, seemingly sensing that I wanted to be alone.

We embraced and he was gone. I was asleep on my make-shift bed before I heard his car start.

Note from the Author

Montbretia appears in several of my books, including the Boniface series. You can find out about her further exploits by joining my readers group.

When you join my readers group I'll send you my introductory library, for free. The introductory library is a collection of books to introduce you to some of the characters and the worlds of my books. And of course, as a member of my readers' group, I'll let you know about my new releases.

Join my readers' group and get your free books here: simoncann.com/readers.

About the Author

Simon Cann is the author of the Boniface, Montbretia Armstrong, and Leathan Wilkey books.

In addition to his fiction, Simon has written a range of music-related and business-related books, including the How to Make a Noise series, the most widely ready series about synthesizer sound programming, and Made it in China, about entrepreneurs building businesses in China. He has also worked as a ghostwriter on a number of books.

Before turning full-time to writing, Simon worked as a management consultant, where his clients included aeronautical, pharmaceutical, defense, financial services, chemical, entertainment, and broadcasting companies.

He lives in London.